Creak

Chapter One

Wichita, Kansas
Saturday 30th August 2014
18:13 p.m.

A sigh passed my lips, followed by another throaty agreement while the female on the other end of the line continued her long-winded speech.

I loved Jayne, but she embodied the definition of irritating, and if I had to talk to her much longer, I would start knocking my head against the wall.

"Nikki, are you even listening to me?"

I opened my eyes. The orange light of the setting sun was coming through the window to glide across my ceiling. My focus then fixed on the silver nub sitting in the centre of the overhead fan, which continued to turn above my bed.

"Of course I'm listening to you." I unravelled the chunk of brown hair I had idly wrapped around my index finger. "But I've already told you, I'm not going to Kimber's party."

"Why, because of James?"

My ex-boyfriend's smug face filled my mind and caused acidic pain to slice through my chest. "He's one of the reasons," I replied, while twisting onto my side.

"Look, I've played the supportive friend long

enough, but clearly, it isn't getting me anywhere."

That urge to snort—had to resist it. Did Jayne even know what 'supportive' meant; you know, outside of the purpose of push-up bras.

"He's a dick, and you have been moping and completely unsociable all summer. Enough is enough, Nikki. It's been five months since you guys broke up. I get that cramming for your finals pulled you through the early stages, but you've graduated from the oh so wonderful Wichita State University and now you're back in the real world. It's time to get on with the rest of your life. You can't hide in your house forever. You've missed so much—"

"I haven't been hiding." I mean, okay, I had to admit I hadn't partaken in many, if not any, of the summer events my friends attend every year. But why make it such a big deal? I should be allowed off the hook for having my ass dumped.

"Yes, you have, and it's wrong. He should be in hiding. Do you know how many times I've had to stop Kacey from kicking his ass?"

A sigh escaped me. "I haven't been in the mood to go out, all right? As for James, I don't know if I'll kill him or end up crying if I see him."

Jayne unfortunately wasn't the faithful type, so no matter what I said, she would hardly understand how upset I felt that the guy I had been dating for four years had been cheating on me for two.

"Do both, do nothing, I don't care. Just stop hiding."

"I know. And I know he isn't worth the time or the effort in either case, but I just can't trust myself around him at the moment."

James had been my first serious relationship, and everything had seemed fine until we got to university. I could blame myself for being busy, but it would be complete bullshit. He got the same attention from me that he always had, but for some reason, that wasn't enough anymore.

"He cheated on you. He should be hiding in his little hole, while you come out and have fun with your friends."

Irritating as hell, but she had a point. "I know."

"We need to get you laid."

Despite the fact she couldn't see my face, my brow furrowed in response. "How is that going to help?"

"Rebound sex is exactly what you need right now. Sweaty, dirty, work-your-frustration-out sex. In fact, I have the perfect guy in mind—"

I jolted up at the sound of a firm tapping at the window to see Kacey's sun kissed face, his shades resting at the edge of his long nose, baby blue eyes fixed on me.

My hand travelled to my thumping heart. "You ass."

"Bitch?"

"Not you, Jayne." I climbed off my bed. "Kay and Ty are here."

"Speak of the devil, and his sexy ass will most definitely appear."

My steps faltered. "I'm so pretending that I didn't even hear you go there."

Her husky laughter filled my ear. "And I so can't believe you haven't already gone there. What's wrong with you?"

"Er, they're my best friends."

"What are friends for, but to help each other get through bad times and have multiple orgasms?"

"Something is seriously wrong with you."

"Look who's talking. You have two hot guys at your beck and call, and you haven't even fooled around with either of them. For shame, Nikki."

"We've been friends since childhood."

"Shit changes. I'm actually willing to bet money that they have both fantasized about fucking you since the age of sixteen."

My throat dried, and although I hated to admit it, the thought that they might see me in such a way had my stomach in multiple knots. "I doubt that."

"They have dicks, and you're delish. Trust me, they've thought about tapping your fine ass on a multitude of occasions."

Another knock echoed. At the window, the usual mischievous smile formed on Kacey's face. He crooked his finger in a come-hither fashion, and my bones turned to jelly.

I cleared my throat. Heat licked my cheeks. "I'm hanging up now."

Her laughter fanned the fire rolling beneath the surface of my skin.

"Ask them. I'm sure they would both be happy to fuck you senseless."

"Bye." I hung up and placed my cell phone on my dresser.

Taking a deep breath, I walked over to the window and flicked the latches. My hands trembled as I pushed the frame up and locked it into place. I folded my arms across my chest and stepped out of the way. "You know, I do have a front door."

Kacey snorted and climbed through the medium gap.

"If I used your door, how would I ever accidentally catch you getting undressed?" He straightened and looked down at me. "Be sensible now."

His baby blues gleamed as he made the usual flirtatious evaluation of me, and as always, a giddy flutter stroked the walls of my stomach.

I really wish I could blame the vast fluctuation in my heartbeat and the sudden flash of heat over my body on Jayne winding me up, but truth be told, for the last couple of years, I may have had the odd thought about sleeping with Kacey, and Tyler. I usually entertained these thoughts after consuming a mass amount of alcohol, which always got me in the mood and made me feel like doing something stupid. But then, those thoughts were still there at sombre moments, too—dancing in the darkest and most forbidden corners of my mind.

It really didn't help that Kacey looked like one hell of a tempting package, the type of guy you wanted to do nasty things to, in exchange for finding out what that wicked glint in his eyes was all about. Or the fact that Tyler had the whole dark hair and dark bottomless eyes going for him. Not to mention the broody "I-will-take-my-time-and-then-hold-you-all-night-long" appeal.

But as tempting as the thought of being crazy with two guys I trusted seemed —and sweet merciful Jesus, the urge to throw caution to the wind got stronger with each year that went by—I really didn't want to lose my best friends.

With my hands on my hips, I looked past him. "And what's your excuse?"

Tyler's slender lips curved as he slipped through the open window. "We've been using your window as our front door for fifteen years. Old habits are hard to break."

"What took you so long?"

"Kacey was being picky," Tyler replied while he shut and locked the window.

"I wanted to watch a good comedy, for a change, instead of all this slasher and space shit you two watch all the time."

I glanced at Tyler. "Uh-oh, what have we ended up with?"

He reached inside his jacket and retrieved two DVDs from the inner pocket. "Just Go With It and Insidious."

I took the films off him.

"Adam Sandler?" I glanced at Kacey. "You're forgiven. Good choice with Insidious, Ty. It's meant to be jumpy, freaky."

"Was that Jayne, by any chance?" Kacey walked over to my bed and jumped onto it. "Please don't say you agreed to go to Kimber's party this weekend, because I may have to spank you."

I arched an eyebrow at him. "You're not going?"

He snorted and cushioned his head with his arms. "You're damn right I'm not."

The DVDs ended up on my dresser and my steps took me to the end of the bed. "Do I want to know why?"

"I'm not going because it's the same shitty party

every year, with the same douche-bags."

Tyler strolled over to my desk and took a seat in my computer chair. "Plus we didn't think you would want to go because, well—"

Kacey's jaw tensed. "I swear I would have kicked his ass already, but Jayne is always there."

"As tempting as the idea is, I don't want you to hurt James." I folded my arms across my chest and glanced at the floor. "He isn't worth it."

"He ain't worth shit, but it would sure make me feel a whole lot better to rearrange his annoying face."

"I guess it's a good thing it isn't about making you feel better, then," Tyler commented. "How are you holding up?"

A laugh bubbled out and my gaze flew up to him. "I'm not going to break, Ty."

"Course you ain't." Kacey slid his sunglasses on top of his head, pushing back his thick, chestnut curls. He smiled at me. "Our girl's tough."

So tough I'd been hiding in my house all summer like Jayne had said. Way to go, me.

"Well, if we're skipping the party, do you wanna go to the movies or something?"

"We got a better idea." Kacey propped himself up on his elbows. "What would you say to a trip to Omaha?"

My glance flipped between the two of them, my eyes widening. "I'd have to ask, why do you want to go out of state?"

Kacey shrugged. "Change of scenery, and new meat."

I rolled my eyes. "You're so gross."

A girlish shriek left my lips as he sprung forward and grabbed me by the waist. The next thing I knew, he'd trapped me between his arms, chest, and legs, with my face buried in my bedding.

"It's the Heat Wave Festival. Last big event of summer," Tyler explained.

"Look, the gates open at nine next Friday morning, but naturally, it's a little too late for me to book time off work. So we were thinking—"

"That we'd make a trip out of it," Tyler intercepted. "Head on up after Kacey finishes work, scrounge some tickets off a seller—"

I twisted onto my back and pushed my hair out of my face.

"Get wasted and generally have an awesome time," Kacey added.

"Then we hit the road Sunday morning, and we're back home by the afternoon."

"Simple and safe. What do you say?"

I looked up at Kacey. "It seems like a waste of time. What if we can't get tickets?"

He rolled his eyes. "God, you have gotten so boring since you've been to Uni."

"Have not." I punched him in the ribs, scowling when he began chuckling.

"Come on, Nikki, I'll make it worth your while."

I tensed at the feel of his hand slipping under my T-shirt. The rough pads of his fingertips danced lightly across my stomach and his gentle touch sent hot electricity running straight down to my clit.

"You've got nothing I want," I lied with a quip of my

lips.

Kacey just grinned at me and continued running his fingers back and forth along my abdomen. It felt rather soothing, or it had until his pinkie skimmed the top of my jeans, and I had to bite my inner cheek to keep from arching. I couldn't even remember the last time James had touched me in such a simple way. . . .

"It would be good for you to get out of town," Tyler stated. "Or if it's not so good, then like Kay said, at least it will just be a change of scenery for two days."

"Just come with us and then, we promise we will leave you alone to mope for at least two weeks before trying to drag your cute ass somewhere else."

I looked between them both. "You really want to go?"

"Hell, yes."

Tyler shrugged. "It could be fun. Plus, as much as I love popcorn, we kinda have a movie night every week, anyway."

I sighed. "Fine, but on one condition."

"Yes, you can give me a blow job. I am so completely fine with that."

I batted Kacey's hand away, before I became too comfortable with it roaming lower than my stomach. "You wish."

"I do. I really, really do, baby girl."

I flipped him off and pushed myself up. "Jayne, Shauna, and Craig are coming with us."

Kacey groaned and let his head fall back. "Not Craig."

I shifted round and faced him. "Since when have you

had a problem with him?"

Tyler smiled. "Since he and Shauna blew two hours in the guest room at Mark's."

My eyes widened and I tilted my head to the side. "You and Shauna?"

"We got drunk." Kacey scrubbed his hands down his face. "We were horny, and hey, shit happens."

Clearly, I had missed more than I thought over the last few months.

"Well, those are my conditions. Jayne has just spent twenty minutes busting my butt for being a recluse all summer and ignoring everyone. She will be pissed if I run off with you two to go to a festival."

Tyler chuckled and spun round on my computer chair. "Looks like you're going to have to behave yourself. Think you can manage that, Kay?"

"Yeah, I think I can ignore Shauna and her bitch boyfriend for one weekend."

"Great." I smiled at Tyler. "I will run the idea past the others tomorrow. Otherwise, I guess that means we're spending next weekend in Omaha."

Chapter Two

Silver Creek, Missouri
Friday 5th September 2014
22:48 p.m.

We had lost the sun about three hours ago, and the helpful lights of the other cars and the freeway about an hour after.

We'd all agreed to cut through the small town of Silver Creek in order to knock an hour off our journey; a decision I was beginning to regret.

My face had been practically glued to the window for the last hour, trying to figure out where the night sky ended and the ground began. It was pitch-black out there. Not night painted in a mixture of dark hues with the added colour jumping out once in a while—this was total and complete darkness, the type that seemed to move with us. The half moon above and the clear blanket of stars had become our only indication that we hadn't just driven into a tunnel with no end.

The headlights of Kacey's green camper van continued to guide us along the narrow road and further toward Silver Creek, which I still wasn't sure if we had arrived in or not.

In the dim orange glow of the overhead light, I turned toward Kacey. The blood had drained from his knuckles due to the grip he had on the steering wheel, his plump lips set in a firm line. He was pissed. I would even say, livid. Which meant only one thing—we had gotten lost.

"Kay?" I said softly. "You might as well pull over."

His eyes narrowed to slits. His focus stuck to the ongoing road. "No."

"It's pitch black. There's no lights anywhere, no sign of life. Pull over and let's all spend the night in the van. We can set off early tomorrow, when we can actually see, and figure out where the hell we are exactly."

He may have been a mechanic, but puncturing a tire or crashing into a tree was the last thing any of us needed.

"There's a Motel."

I peered at the surrounding darkness with wide eyes. "I don't see one."

He turned the sat nav and pointed at a small blue square. "It should be here somewhere."

I stared at the small screen and then back out the front window. Who the hell would put a motel out here? Then again, I suppose if it's a small trade town, and people did cut through like we're doing . . . .

"There's the fucker," Kacey declared and put his foot on the gas.

The van jolted as we went over a bump in the road, and a groan came from the back.

"What the hell, Kay?" I turned to see Tyler rubbing the back of his head and looking at us through hooded lids.

"Are we there yet?" he asked.

I shook my head. "We're lost."

"We're not lost," Kacey stated sharply. "I came down the right route. It's just fucking taking forever because I have to go at a tortoise pace because some stupid asshole didn't think about putting up lights on this shitty back road."

Tyler yawned. "So, we're lost?"

Kacey growled. "We'll stop here, and set off in the morning."

I looked back out at the road and the speck of light that had suddenly emerged from nowhere growing bigger and bigger, finally forming in to a readable size and shape.

The tall sign to the 'Creek Motel' flickered in the on-going darkness. The faulty light to the isolated establishment appeared to be the only indication that actual people lived in the area, and after an hour of nothing but darkness, the sight caused a pop of relief to tickle my stomach.

Kacey slowed and turned the van into the small parking lot.

Apart from the two cars sitting along the front of the L-shaped building, the only other sign that the motel operated came from the dull light seeping through the curtains of a few rooms. The van filled with soft groans as Tyler woke up the others and Kacey manoeuvred into a free space.

"Are you kidding me?" Disgust leaked into Jayne's sleep-filled voice.

Kacey scrubbed his hands down his face. "What did you expect, the Hilton?"

"I expected to be in a packed parking lot with tons of people, and lights and loud music." She yawned.

"Where are we?"

He cut the engine and slid out of his seatbelt. "We're stopping here for the night."

"Where is here?"

"We're in Silver Creek."

"Yeah, which is just another name for 'we're in the middle of fucking nowhere'."

Kacey twisted in his seat. "Look, it's too dark. So we're stopping here. We'll set off in the morning and be at the festival in no time. Deal with it."

Dry laughter scraped her throat. "You're so grumpy. Jesus. It's not my fault we had to set off at half past six. We should have set off tomorrow morning."

Kacey popped his jaw and slid a look at me. "I'll go get us signed in, shall I?"

"I'll come with you." I pushed the door open and climbed out of the van.

I pulled my jacket tightly around me as we made our way across the rough ground toward the entrance. In the silence, each small gust of wind whipping around the solitary building could be heard.

I followed Kacey through the open doorway in to the dingy, snug reception, which had bare brick walls with old photographs lining them and a heavily worn and scratched wooden floor. Kacey hit the small brass bell sitting on the reception desk and we both stood looking at the closed office door.

"Do you think the manager has gone to sleep?" My glance slid to him; he squinted in some weak attempt to see through the misted glass of the door.

"Not much else to do round here, so it wouldn't

surprise me." He hit the bell again. "There's light flickering in there though, so he or she is probably watching a bit of porn."

"Why do you have to assume its porn?"

He looked at me and shrugged. "If I got stuck out here, sleeping and jacking off would be the best way to pass the time."

"You have serious issues." I shook my head and looked back at the office door as it opened.

A scrawny, middle-aged woman with faded brown hair stopped in front of us, her grey, beady eyes almost glacial.

She studied us both. "How can I help you?"

"Hey, yeah we would like three rooms, if that's possible?" Kacey asked.

The corners of her mouth curled and a spark of delight lit her cold eyes.

For some reason, the sight caused a shiver to run down my spine.

"It sure is. We charge only for the rooms, and they're thirty dollars a night." She glanced out into the dark lot. "You kids lost?"

"That depends. Are we in Silver Creek?" Kacey asked as he pulled out his wallet.

"You sure are."

"Then no, it's just a little too dark for us to be driving." He placed ninety dollars on the counter. "There you go."

"Thank you." She took hold of the money before she turned and walked over to the wooden cabinet on the wall, collecting three sets of keys from there.

"I'm afraid we only have rooms with double beds. I trust that won't be an issue?" she asked as she walked back over to us.

Kacey grinned. "Not at all."

"Great." She placed the keys on the counter and then tapped the open page of the guest book. "If you'd just sign your name?"

"Sure."

"If you have any questions or anything, you just pick up your phone and hit one and then hash and it will direct you straight to me—I'm Sarah, by the way—or my husband, Ernie."

"Do you own this establishment?" I asked.

"Goin' on eight years now."

"It's lovely, and we're so lucky that you're here. Otherwise, it would have been a crammed night in the van."

Sarah's smile grew impossibly wide, revealing a full mouth of crooked teeth. "Oh, heck, we couldn't have that now, could we?"

My own smile faltered as uncertainty twisted in my stomach. I couldn't take my focus off the small woman standing before me, and the longer I stared at her smile, the more I felt like a tiny fish standing in the presence of a hungry shark.

Kacey placed the pen on the book. "There we go."

"Well, that's everything." She looked between us. "You all have a lovely night's sleep."

"We will, thank you." Kacey grabbed the keys from the counter.

Sarah tilted her head and stared at me. "Good night."

"Night," I replied softly.

Kacey wrapped his arm around my waist and we left the reception. I glanced over my shoulder as we headed back to the camper van, and unease washed over me at the sight of Sarah standing at the window, watching us. The smile had vanished from her face, her gaze fixated on us. A stern expression clutched her face.

"She's watching us."

"She probably doesn't trust us." Kacey gave my waist a gentle squeeze. "No doubt she's thinking we will keep her other customers up all night."

"She gives me the creeps." I glanced around the lot. "This whole place is giving me the creeps."

"Are we good?" Tyler handed me my bags once we stopped by the van.

"Yeah, fifteen dollars each, so y'all can pay me back when we get home." He threw a set of keys at Craig. "You two love birds get your own room, which leaves . . . huh, Tyler and Jayne, and you and me, baby."

I looked up at him, knowing I should tell him to go to Hell, but staying with him would have made me feel better. Something didn't feel right about the place.

Kacey chuckled. "Holy shit. You are actually freaking out, aren't you?"

"Freaking about what?" A hint of concern licked Tyler's tone.

"She thinks the manager is creepy."

"She is." I turned back to look at the window of the reception to find Sarah had gone.

Jayne plucked a set of keys from Kacey's hand. "Well, no offence, Ty, but you really don't do it for me.

So Nikki and I will be sharing, and you two get to continue with your bromance in private."

"Believe me, I'm not offended," Tyler replied with a slight twitch of his lips.

"Whatever." Jayne headed over to the ongoing strip of windows and doors. "Are you coming, Nikki?"

My gaze flicked from Tyler to Kacey.

"We shouldn't stay here," I told them as I hefted my bag on to my shoulder and followed Jayne.

* * *

Images flicker across the screen, and I watch without really seeing. The light from the television floods only half of my darkened room, creating shadows as it weaves round my belongings. Apart from the low hum of chatter from the programme, the room is silent. My world is quiet; it's always quiet. Always lonely. Never anything to do. Never anyone to play with . . .

I lift my head from the pillow as a distant rumbling catches my attention. A car? Possibly, but so many people pass through. Never stopping. Never staying. It makes them angry. It makes me sad.

I sit up as the rumble grows louder. Definitely not a car. The vehicle sounds bigger, the engine different.

Slowing, easing, turning . . . Tires crunch along gravel. White light flashes through my curtains and the growl of a nearby engine strokes my eardrums. Anticipation kicks in. I dare not move.

The engine dies. The air catches in my throat, and my heart begins to thump.

Visitors.

I stumble off the bed at the sound of metal creaking—doors being slammed shut—to creep to the window, brush the fabric to the side, and peer out into the darkness. It is dark out there, but the warm light from the reception seeps across half of the lot. I can make out the forms of a man and a woman making their way inside.

Are they lost? Asking for directions? Wanting to spend the night?

Curiosity spikes, and I find myself glued to the spot waiting for them to emerge in to the night once more.

Another door opens. The sound of voices catches my attention. More people climbing out of a van.

People. I hadn't seen so many strangers in a very long time. The sight excites me.

They will be happy if these visitors stay. They will be very happy. I could play. They will let me play.

The group by the van turns as the man and woman leave the reception. My focus drifts back to them, to the man's arm which is wrapped across the woman's waist.

Touching. Touching is nice. Touching feels good. I like touching.

The tinkle of metal rings as the man throws a pair of keys at one of his companions.

A shudder races through me. I fist the curtain, my smile wide.

They are staying. I'm not alone anymore.

✶ ✶ ✶

My unease turned with each step, and a creeping sensation wriggled up my back; like someone watching me. My stomach clenched at the thought and I found myself checking the line of windows for faces.

Get a grip, girl. It's just a motel. A creepy, isolated motel.

"Number eleven . . . ah, here we are. Number twelve," Jayne said as I stopped beside her. "You have to know that Kacey wants you. I mean, come on."

She unlocked the door and we slipped in to the room.

I brushed my hand against the wall, looking for the light switch. "Jayne, please. I'm not in the mood for another one of your twisted pep-talks."

Plus I was two seconds away from leaving Jayne on her own and staying with Tyler and Kacey; bad idea in itself. I had to be tired. I'd spent the last hour with next to no light and staring out in to darkness. Maybe the brighter light of the motel reception altered stranger's faces, making them look unwelcoming? Yeah, that had to be it.

Or maybe I'm crazy?

"God, why are you so cranky?"

"It's been a long journey."

"You should have got some sleep."

I bit my lip to stop myself from making a "no duh" comment.

My fingers brushed over the plastic switch, and I flicked it down.

Jayne closed the red door, and we both stood and evaluated the room. To be honest, I had been expecting something a lot worse. Despite the dullness, the place actually appeared clean and neat. The flowery paper with shades of peach and red had evidently matched the colour of the somewhat worn carpet and curtains at one time. The bedside tables matched the pine dresser which sat against the wall, with a TV on top facing the bed.

Jayne wandered over to the half-open door and flicked on the light to the bathroom.

"Are there any cockroaches in there?"

"It actually smells like sanitizer in here. I'm glad, because the last thing I want is to catch something."

I rolled my eyes and dropped my bag on the floor. Moving over to the bed, I lifted one of the pillows to my nose and sniffed. The distinct scent of soap powder hit me. Anything else, I could have lived with, but sleeping in sheets a stranger had used repulsed me.

"Right, I'm getting a shower." Jayne threw her red suitcase on the bed and began removing her T-shirt. "And then, we're going next door to see if we can have some fun in this place."

I stared at her as if she had just slapped me on the face. "Explain what the heck you mean by that."

She unzipped her large handbag and pulled out two bottles of Jack Daniels. "You owe me some fun."

"I don't owe you anything."

"Fine. You owe yourself some fun, which is why I'm guessing you agreed to go to this stupid festival in the first place. Plus, if this shit-hole is giving you the chills, you have clearly been held up inside your house for too long. So you need a drink." She put the bottles on the bedside table and pulled out a stack of plastic cups.

28 | Elizabeth Morgan

"Now, I need you to go and grab a couple of cans of Diet Coke from the vending machine I saw outside."

God, it annoyed me how Jayne's bullshit somehow always made sense.

With a sigh, I threw the cream-coloured pillow down. "Anything else I can get you, Your Majesty?"

At least if I had a drink, I might be able to get drunk enough to forget that the manager looked like she would eat me.

"As many bags of Doritos as you can get." She began unbuttoning her jeans. "We got to make the most of what we've got."

I shook my head and grabbed my purse from my bag.

"Lock the door behind you," she said as she wandered into the bathroom.

After grabbing the key, I stepped back outside and locked the door to our room, standing quietly for a moment, my gaze wandering to the reception and then back across the empty lot.

Who the hell would want to run a motel out here?

Perhaps I was being stupid. The place was just quiet, and perhaps folks round here appeared scary because they desperately needed the business?

"Running away already?"

I jumped at the sound of Tyler's voice. Hand on heart, I turned and scowled at him as he shut the door to his room. "No, I'm going to stock up on supplies, because apparently, we're coming to yours and having a party."

Tyler's eyebrows arched in unison.

"She's brought booze. I just need to grab some

snacks and then look out, we're coming round."

"I guess it beats shit TV."

We began walking along the sheltered walkway. "Where are you running off to?"

"I was just going to raid the vending machines myself." Tyler looked at the door to Craig and Shauna's room. "I take it we're leaving the happy couple to enjoy their own company?"

"Somehow, I don't think Shauna will want to be in a room with Kacey when he's been drinking. Not again, anyway."

A smile spread on his lips. "I guess not."

We took a couple more steps before he tapped me with his elbow. His focus shifted between his feet and the wall ahead. "So, how are you, really?"

"I'm fine. My eyes must have been playing tricks on me after an hour of staring at nothing."

"I actually meant in general. You might be able to fool Kacey with a couple of brush offs, but I know you better than that."

My eyebrow arched as I looked up at him. "Oh, you do, do you?"

"I'd like to think so." He shrugged. "Look, I get that you don't want to talk in front of Kacey because he rants and makes threats. And although I completely agree with him on the fact that James is a total dick and deserves an ass kicking, it doesn't mean that I'm going to do the same because I think that's what you want to hear."

"All right, you really want to know how I feel?" With a sigh, I folded my arms across my chest and stared at the wall ahead. "I feel stupid that I let myself get played."

"You didn't let yourself get played. You weren't to know."

"I should have."

"You'd been with James for two years before you both went to Uni. It shocked us all that he could do such a thing. He seemed like a decent guy."

A dry laugh escaped me. "Yeah, he did, and yet, he turned out to be a complete tool."

"Kacey's a tool. James is a fucking idiot for not realizing how amazing you are."

Heat blossomed in my cheeks as we stopped next to the vending machines.

"I promise you, he'll regret it."

"Somehow, I doubt that." I unzipped my purse. "The stupid thing is, things didn't feel right. Things between us felt off, and I just—" I sighed and slipped a couple of dollars into the machine.

"You just?"

"Why didn't I do anything about it?" I punched two buttons and a bag of Doritos fell to the bottom. "Why didn't I sit down sooner and talk with him?"

Tyler moved to the drink machine and slipped a couple of coins in the slot. "If he'd been honest and said he had been seeing someone else—"

"Then it would have been over a lot sooner." I wouldn't have been able to stay with him knowing he had cheated on me; not that he would've wanted that, anyway. It had been pretty clear that we were over the moment I finally confronted him about everything.

"Did you love him, Nikki?" He pressed a couple of

buttons and then looked at me. His dark gaze searched my face. "I know you were crazy about him in the beginning, and that you were upset when you found out he'd cheated. But did you?"

"If I really did love him…" I slipped another two dollars into the machine. "I would have tried to work it out, fight for him even if it seemed pointless. But I didn't. I hate that he lied, and that he'd been fucking about with someone else behind my back. I hate the fact that I slept with him—"

His jaw tensed as he slipped more money into the machine. "You didn't know."

"And a part of me hates the fact that he chose her over me, but I know I wouldn't have stayed with him either way." I punched another two numbers. "I think… I think I'm actually relieved. Is that bad?" A second bag of Doritos joined the other in the tray below. "Should I feel so relieved after four years of being with him?"

He bent down and collected the two bottles from the tray. "It depends on whether you were happy, I guess."

"He used to go into moods over the most ridiculous things, and he would always come out with stuff that would just . . . God, get under my skin. At times, he behaved like a child."

"And yet, you stayed with him."

I leant down and pushed open the flap to the machine. "I think that I believed I loved him. I know love is hard, but sometimes, I really felt like I needed to push myself to give a damn with him, and that's not right, is it?"

I grabbed the bags of Doritos and straightened.

"What the hell is wrong with me?" I turned and

looked at him. "I had to have been so thick to just stay with him, because . . . I don't even know. I don't know why I stayed with him, and I don't know why I've hidden in my house for the last couple of months like a complete idiot."

He reached out. His fingertips brushed against my cheek as he slid my hair behind my ear. I welcomed the gesture more than I cared to admit, and it took every fibre of my being to stay still and not lean into his touch.

"You're human, and therefore prone to make mistakes. Like dating a complete dick-head."

"Yeah, well, hopefully, it's not a mistake I will make again."

The smile on his lips softened as he ran his knuckles along my jaw. "You won't. You just need to realize that there are better guys around."

I gulped as his thumb skimmed the bottom of my lip. Heat wrapped around my spine. "Are there?"

He lifted my chin slightly. "I'll always be here for you, you know that, right?"

I nodded and my breath hitched as he leaned in. My eyelids fluttered shut of their own will, and my lips parted. My heart thundered in my ears. I leaned in, caught in between protesting and beating him to the chase . . . He pressed a kiss on my cheek.

Disappointment and shame collided in my gut as he pulled away and smiled at me.

"Well, don't forget it."

I forced a smile. "As if I would."

"Are you done stocking up?"

"I just need to get some Diet Coke for Her Highness."

"All right. Well, I will see you in a few minutes, then." He turned and made his way back down the walkway.

I leaned against the vending machine and shook my head. "What the hell is wrong with me?"

✶ ✶ ✶

I slip the broken segment of wood from the door and press my eye to the hole, watching as the two women speak, as the one with fire for hair removes her top. A familiar heat awakens in my body as her slender fingers pop the button on her jeans.

I hate when they wear trousers.

I tense as she turns. My heart stops for a single second in fear that she will catch me watching, but instead, she makes her way into the bathroom. She pushes her jeans down her long legs to reveal a string of red lining the base of her spine. The material runs between the crack of her perked ass, and as she bends forward to pull the jeans from her ankles, the material slides against her beautiful pussy.

My cock swells in the confinements of my jogging pants.

I dig my nails into the wooden frame and suck in a ragged breath. She removes the scrap of material in one easy glide and climbs into the shower stall, rolling the misted glass screen into place. A pop of pressure and the rush of water echoes within the small room.

A husky moan resonates in her throat. The sound makes my cock throb.

Pushing my pants to my knees, I grab my cock and begin to pump it. My gaze wanders over her blurry form, watching the way her hands slide over her wet hair and body.

She is beautiful.

I want her.

I move my hand back and forth along my length, squeezing, while I imagine what it would be like to be inside her. She will spread her thighs for me. She will be tight around my shaft as I slip deep inside her cunt. She will moan beneath me as I pound her sweet little pussy.

I tighten my grip and fuck my hand harder at the thought of how much she wants me.

It has been too long since I have felt the wet heat of a woman.

I will not deny her. I will make my little redhead scream.

Chapter Three

01:12 a.m.

I tipped the plastic back, but no matter how hard I shook the flimsy cup, no liquid came out.

"My drink has gone."

Across the room, Tyler and Kacey sat with their backs against the wall.

Kacey lifted the remaining bottle of Jack Daniels up and shook it. The final quarter of amber liquid splashed against its glass walls and a predatory smile emerged on his face.

"You want it? Come and get it, baby girl."

His response was husky and a little drawled. I couldn't help but think if he used that tone during sex. The thought made my panties damp. I looked down at Jayne who lay on her side. She wiggled her eyebrows at me and started laughing while kicking my side with her red-painted toes.

I tried my best to scowl at her before throwing such a look at Kacey. "No way. I know what you do to drunken females."

"You want me, though. Just admit it," he replied with a crooked grin. "I could have your world spinning faster than Jack and coke and you know it."

I snorted a laugh. "I know nothing."

I crossed my legs and clenched my thighs as the

alcohol-fuelled ache in my core began to pulse. My nipples tightened under his heavy gaze, and I had to fight the urge to squirm on the spot. Pulling my attention from him, I looked over at Tyler, and pouted. "My drink's gone and Kay's being a dick."

A grin curved his lips and a shiver ran down my spine. Kacey grinning looked sexy, but there was something toe-curling about Tyler mirroring such a smile.

God, I need to stop drinking, and like, right now.

"I knew you liked me better."

"It's got nothing to do with liking you best, and you know it."

"Bullshit." Tyler grabbed the bottle from Kacey's hand and crawled over to me.

Kacey gave a sharp laugh. "She wouldn't have asked if she knew you—"

"Shut up," Tyler grunted as he twisted and sat beside me.

"Wait a minute, if I knew what?" With a hooded gaze, I glanced between them. "What don't I know?"

"That Tyler is totally in love with you." Jayne giggled and put her hand over her mouth. "Oops, did I just say that out loud?"

Nervous laughter slipped from my lips. "Say what?"

"God, you're such a bitch." Kacey scrunched his cup up and threw it at her.

"Says you. You're his best friend and you're on the verge of tattling on him. Who the fuck does that?"

My eyes widened as I glanced between her and Kacey, and then at Tyler as he took the cup from my hand.

"Are they joking?" I asked as I twisted to face him.

"It's the truth."

I glared at Kacey. "I'm not talking to you. I'm talking to Ty."

Kacey shrugged. "You ain't going to get an answer from him. He's too chicken shit to admit it."

"Or maybe I just think there are moments for such conversations," Tyler snapped. His gaze pinned Kacey to the opposite wall as he handed me my refill.

"She's not with James anymore, so what the fuck's the deal, man?"

"The deal is she's upset about what he did and she needs time."

"In other words, you're avoiding telling her. Surprise fucking surprise."

"It's got nothing to do with you."

"It has everything to do with me, especially when I've had to put up with you doing gooey eyes at her for the last eight fucking years."

"What, and you think now is a good time to tell her? Now, when she is drunk? You think this is how I wanted to fucking tell her?" Tyler put the bottle on the floor and smacked his forehead with the palm of his hand. "Oh, wait, who the fuck am I talking to? The guy who prefers to fuck every female he has an actual friendship with, and if they're drunk, bonus."

"At least, I'm not a chicken shit. I don't think you had any intention of telling her."

I slammed my cup on the floor, ignoring the liquid spilling onto my hand. "How about we just stop pretending that I'm not in the fucking room, huh? Would that be okay for one damn minute?"

Gripping the side of the bed, I pushed myself to my feet and glared at Kacey. "You're a dick, and I hope you genuinely know that, and you—" I looked at Tyler."—I don't even know what to say."

He sighed. "That's fine, because I don't want you to say anything."

"Is it true?"

"Would it matter?"

"Maybe." I folded my arms across my chest. "You never said anything."

He pushed himself off the floor and faced me. "You've been in a relationship—"

"Before me and James, you never said anything."

"You're my best friend, and although some people would gladly—and literally—fuck such a relationship…" he gave Kacey a pointed look. "I don't want to lose you as a friend."

"Aw."

"Shut up, Jayne," I grunted, not daring to take my focus off Tyler. "You wouldn't lose me. You can't help how you feel."

Jayne's high-pitched giggle filled the room. "Oh my god, this is seriously better than watching 90210."

"But you could never feel the same, right?" Tyler asked.

I opened my mouth, only to shut it again. The room felt like a spinning top, my legs like rubber.

A flicker of pain flashed across Tyler's face, and the sight made my chest clench.

"It's fine, Nikki. I already know the answer."

How could he know the answer, when I didn't even know it? Just hours ago, he'd nearly kissed me, and I had wanted him to. Surely, that meant something, didn't it?

I turned and began walking toward the door. "I need to go lie down."

"I'll come with you," Jayne said.

I didn't wait for her, or give Ty or Kay a chance to say anything else. I left the room as steadily as I could despite my legs feeling wobbly and the fact that I was bobbing from side to side. Fumbling for the key that I had wedged in my pocket, I pulled it out and aimed at the lock.

"Nice going, boys." Jayne laughed as she stumbled through the doorway.

I got the door unlocked on my third try and left Jayne to close it as I walked straight to the bathroom and dropped before the toilet. Throwing the lid open, I allowed the six cups of Jack and cola to leave my stomach, only vaguely aware of the room door closing as I collapsed against the wall and groaned.

"You okay, girl?"

"I honestly don't know."

I listened to her unsteady footfalls as she moved around the bed. Her giggling sounded like pins being shaken in a glass jar, and the noise caused my temples to throb. I pulled my legs to my chest and pressed my head to my knees.

"I honestly can't believe Kay outed Ty like that. He's such a shit-head."

My brow furrowed. "You outed Ty."

"Whatever. Someone would have said something, eventually. He's been in to you since high school. You're so fucking clueless."

"It's Tyler."

"Yeah, and you get along with him. He listens to you, and he is fairly cute. All in all, I would say he's like your ideal guy."

"Is everyone missing the point? We have been friends since the age of nine."

"And you have been friends with Kacey since the age of eleven, but no one points out that tint of red that claims your cheeks every time he flirts with you."

I lifted my head and glared at the open door. "I do not blush when he is being a dick."

"Yeah, you keep telling yourself that." The bedsprings creaked. "What's the big fucking deal, Nikki? If you see both of them as friends and nothing more, then there's no problem. Tell Ty that you're flattered but you don't feel that way about him, and tell Kacey that it is never gonna happen, so to stop being a douche. Problem solved. Case closed."

Fair enough, but it wasn't that simple. What if I did feel something for him? What if I felt something for both of them?

* * * * *

Creak | 41

3:04 a.m.

By the time I had taken a shower and gotten ready for bed, Jayne had fallen fast asleep. I had lain on the mattress staring at the dark ceiling while listening to the sound of the wind travelling down the walkway outside. Not to mention the slight creak of floorboards as the guys moved around in their room. The quietness of the area meant that I could hear Ty and Kacey talking on the other side of the wall, although I didn't have much luck picking up their conversation.

Had Kacey been comforting Tyler? Was Tyler even upset? Or were they just laying into each other?

My chest clenched at the thought that my lack of response may have hurt him. I didn't want to hurt Tyler, but . . . Well, what could I say to him? We had been friends for fifteen years and he had never said anything. And if Jayne was right and he'd been crushing on me since High School... well, eight years and he'd never said one word. He had never even indicated that he may have thought of me as more than a friend.

Something thudded against the wall, and I jolted upright. Kacey's voice grew louder, but I still couldn't make out a word, and the thought that I may have been the topic pissed me off. No way would I let them fall out over me.

Throwing the covers back, I climbed quietly out of bed and grabbed the keys from the bedside table. I tiptoed to the door and unlocked it. Jayne's snores filled the room. Obviously, the whiskey had knocked her on her ass for the night. Perfect.

Opening the door, I slipped outside and locked it

behind me. The floorboards whined beneath my bare feet, and each creak of wood seemed amplified by the deafening silence around me.

Taking a deep breath, I knocked on the door marked thirteen. "It's me."

I wrapped my arms around my stomach as the gentle wind twirled round me, glanced down the length of the empty walk way, and then turned to look at the entrance. In my mind, I could still see Sarah standing at the window watching us like a hawk. The image unnerved me. Hell, the entire motel unnerved me.

I lifted my hand and knocked again, wanting to get my ass back inside before I turned round and found Sarah lurking in some dark corner with a knife.

Lamplight finally filled the covered window, and the door opened. Tyler looked at me. "Hey."

"Can I come in?" I asked while trying to rub the goosebumps from my arms.

He nodded and stepped out of the way. I walked past him and glanced at Kacey who sat on one side of the double bed. My gaze wandered down his chiselled chest and abdomen, stopping when I noticed he wore only tight, black boxer briefs. Heat licked beneath my skin, and the fading buzz from the alcohol stirred in my stomach.

Gulping, I forced myself to look back at Tyler.

"I'm sorry for just walking out earlier, but I don't want you two being bitchy with one another over this whole thing."

"We're not being bitchy," Kacey said defensively.

"I can hear you through the wall." I indicated next door. "I don't want you falling out over this." I looked at Tyler. "I know it can't have been easy telling me —"

"I didn't, technically, tell you."

"No, you didn't, but you should have." I slid a look at Kacey. "And other people need to learn to keep their mouths shut."

"Look, let's just forget about it, okay?"

"I can't, and I—I don't think I want to." I folded my arms across my chest. "You're my best friend, have been forever, and I care about you a lot, but I'm not sure if I feel that way about you."

"I understand."

"But—" I lifted my shoulders. "—there's a possibility I might."

His brow furrowed. "What are you saying?"

If I was going to do this, I had to do it now. Otherwise, things would be awkward, and I didn't want that.

"Earlier, by the vending machines, I thought that you wanted to kiss me, and well, would you have?"

"I think the answer to that is pretty obvious, baby girl," Kacey stated.

I closed the gap between us and placed my trembling hand on Tyler's cheek. "Because I really wish you had."

He stared down at me. Uncertainty flickered across his features. "You're drunk?"

"My head's a little fuzzy, but I'm sober enough to know what I'm on about."

"Nikki, I don't want you doing something you're going to regret just because you're upset over James, or feel guilty—"

"This has nothing to do with him." I leant up and

kissed him.

It was gentle, hardly exciting, but at least my stomach didn't turn.

But he didn't kiss me back.

I pulled away and looked him dead in the eyes. "You've waited eight years. If it doesn't feel right kissing me, then you know keeping quiet was the right thing, and I know that we just had a crazy moment earlier. One kiss and we can stop being curious and just move on."

A small smile appeared as he arched an eyebrow at me. "You've been curious?"

Warmth blossomed in my cheeks. "Maybe."

Kacey chuckled. "I so fucking knew it."

I scowled at him. "Look, we're adults, all right? I don't want us all falling out over this."

"What if it does feel right?"

"Well, there's only one way to find out."

I took a deep breath as Tyler cupped my face. My eyes fluttered shut as his mouth caught mine without hesitation. His tongue flicked against the seam of my lips and a small pop of heat hit the walls of my stomach. I pressed my hands to his chest, my fingers clutching at the material of his T-shirt as I opened up to him.

His tongue slid slowly against my own and the agonizing pace and tease of his gentleness caused my heart to skip. I moved my hands up to his shoulder and neck, then ran my fingers through his black hair as my body melted against him.

He trailed his fingers down my throat, and each tip

sent a different pulse of electricity straight to my toes. His hands fell to my hips and as the pressure of his fingers began to increase with the pace of his demanding lips, my slowly sobering mind began to twist with familiar and forbidden fantasies.

And I wanted to give in to them all.

Why the hell had I ever thought that this would be weird?

We shared everything with one another, so why couldn't we share ourselves? I would never dream of hurting him and I knew Tyler would never hurt me. I trusted him more than I trusted myself and the idea of being locked in his arms while he rocked languidly into me had my entire body thrumming with need.

"Right, I can't watch this shit." Kacey grunted as he got up. "It's one thing getting a hard-on over you, baby girl. The fact that Tyler happens to be in the picture . . . I'm freaking slightly."

I pulled away from Tyler, my breath somewhat shallow as I angled my head so I could glance at Kacey. "I don't want you to go."

Tyler didn't shift his focus from me, and realization slowly slipped across his features. "You weren't just referring to me, right?"

Heat claimed my cheeks. I shook my head, and the smallest dose of guilt began to stab at me.

"I think I could kinda love you both in my own way. I have…sometimes, I have—God, why is this so hard?" I took a deep breath. "There have been times when I've wondered what…across the years, I've sometimes wondered—sometimes, I have considered risking our friendship." I looked over at Kacey. "Do you understand what I am saying to you?"

"You're usually naked when I imagine you saying you want me, but yeah, I understand perfectly."

My jaw tensed. "I hate you sometimes. I hate the way you treat women, and that you can't keep your dick in your pants or your damn mouth shut—"

"But you still want me, right?" He moved closer to me. "When are you going to get it in your head that you're not just some girl, Nikki? You're our girl."

"I want you both," I said quietly, not caring that my voice was trembling along with the rest of my body, or that my cheeks were on fire. "I have for a while."

"If we try this—" Tyler took a deep breath. "—and it doesn't feel right—"

"We'll stop," Kacey promised as he slid his hand beneath my halter neck top and began caressing my skin. "You say it, baby, and we'll stop and forget all about it. No harm. No foul. Friendship intact."

My stomach flipped at the feel of his fingers circling my navel. "And if I don't want to stop?"

An unreadable look crossed Tyler's face, and my heart skipped as Kacey moved behind me. The warmth of his body seeped into my back while his fingers painted trails of heat across my abdomen and along my ribs.

"Then what happens in Silver Creek stays in Silver Creek, unless you decide otherwise." Kacey pressed his lips to my ear. A shiver ran down my neck and spine. "Does that sound fair?"

I closed my eyes and tilted my head to the side as his lips brushed against my jawbone and down the side of my throat. A groan escaped me as his hand closed over my bare breast and he squeezed eagerly. Tyler's hands fell from my hips, and I felt Kacey's right hand splaying on my stomach as he pulled me closer and ground his growing erection into my lower back.

"Yes or no, Nikki?" he asked raggedly. "Tyler ain't the only one whose been fantasizing about this baby, and I hate to remind you but I'm not exactly patient."

I opened my eyes and looked at Tyler, watching as he pulled his T-shirt off and revealed the lean muscles of his abdomen and arms. I reached up and cupped his jaw, idly running my thumb along his bottom lip, while I lifted my left arm and wound it around the back of Kacey's head. I slid my fingers in to his mass of curls and pulled playfully. "Yes."

I angled my head to the side and offered my mouth to Kacey, who claimed it immediately. His tongue slipped against mine as he kissed me so deeply that I became breathless within mere seconds. His left hand released my breast and joined his other hand as he tangled the material of my cotton shorts around his fingers. He pulled away with a grin and pressed his lips against my ear, his voice a sexy rasp that tickled my nerve endings.

"We can't do much with you if you still have your clothes on, can we?"

I unhooked my arm from his neck and gulped as his mouth moved down my throat and then across my shoulder.

I looked back at Tyler as he moved closer to me. My gaze dropped to his pants which lay discarded on the floor, before moving to his impressive erection surrounded by a thick thatch of dark curls. My mouth dried. A blush claimed my entire body. The thought of him thrusting into me made my core tighten and sent moisture flooding between my thighs.

I lifted my arms as he pushed up the material of my top. A shiver spiralled down my spine as the coolness of the room touched my overheated flesh. Kacey pressed open-mouth kisses along my spine while he slowly inched my shorts down my legs. The delicate glide of the material against my skin sent odd quivers of delight trembling through me.

Heated butterflies stroked the walls of my stomach as embarrassment and arousal over my two best friends undressing me fought for dominance. There seemed to be something strangely innocent yet entirely erotic about it, and I found I had to bite the inside of my cheek as I tried not to giggle like a naughty school girl.

I lifted my legs in turn as Kacey eased me out of my shorts. My gaze roamed over Tyler's face as his focus became transfixed on my chest. My nipples tightened under his appreciative observation.

He threw my top to one side and reached out, running the back of his hand over the curve of my right breast. "I always knew you'd be beautiful."

"Beautiful doesn't even cover it," Kacey stated as he ran his hands up the back of my thighs. "Why has it taken so fucking long for us to do this?"

I explored Tyler's chest, tracing the faint curves of muscle. "I guess we didn't trust our friendship enough?"

Tyler slid his hand into my hair and pulled me into a deep kiss. The earlier caution had vanished and although the simple movement of his mouth and the way his tongue brushed against mine remained languid and teasing, the kiss tasted of need—and I wanted it. I wanted their need, because I knew in that moment that I genuinely wanted this, wanted them, and no way would I stop this from happening.

Tyler ran his hands over my ass and I groaned into his mouth as he cupped my thighs and picked me up. His erection pressed against my entrance and my core pulsed with aching need.

"We would never hurt you," he stated breathlessly against my mouth. "Never. I need you to know that."

"I know." I nodded, before leaning in and kissing him again, vaguely aware of us turning, of the whine of the bedsprings as Tyler knelt at the edge and lay me down.

I slid my hands into his hair and arched into him as he dropped his head and kissed his way down my throat and to my breast. He took my left nipple into his mouth. His tongue swirled around the tightening bud while his hands coaxed my thighs open.

The bed dipped beside me, and I turned to see Kacey reclining in a lazy fashion. A cat-like grin claimed his lips as he fisted his thick shaft and began pumping slowly.

An illicit thrill ran through me, and I licked my lips. "Need a hand?"

The wicked glint appeared in his baby blues, and I reached for him. I wrapped my left hand around his silky flesh and began stroking him.

Tyler slid farther down my body. His teeth scorched my abdomen as he spread my thighs wide. My grip on Kacey faltered as Tyler dipped his head between my legs and ran his tongue slowly along my wet slit. I whimpered.

"She likes that, Ty." Kacey twisted onto his side. "I bet she tastes sweet, right?" He wrapped his hand round mine and continued pumping his cock. "Like strawberries and cream."

Tyler moaned, and I wasn't sure if he agreed, protested, or was telling Kacey to shut up. Either way, he continued to lick and suck at my over-sensitive flesh until I panted.

"Oh, God! Right there…right there…."

My mind spun with too many pleas as my body tried to keep up with the twisting sensation in my gut. The feel of Tyler's tongue inside me, mixed with the sound of Kacey's masculine groans, had me dizzy and needy all at once.

It felt like too much was happening, and yet, I wanted more. I wanted to be blown out of my fucking mind, so I would forget about the last couple of months. Hell, the last couple of years.

I tangled my other hand in Tyler's hair and pressed his head closer as he slipped two fingers inside me.

"God, that feels so good." I moaned, rocking my hips uncontrollably against Tyler's onslaught of pleasure.

Kacey' rolled on to his back as I began pumping him harder. "I knew you were sexy, Nikki, but fuck me—"

"I will." I glanced at him, loving the way the muscles in his abdomen and thighs flexed as he fought to hang on. "Just tell me you have condoms with you."

Kacey fisted the sheets. "Who the hell do you think you're talking to here?"

The breath caught in my throat and my hips lifted off the bed as Tyler sucked my nub between his teeth. "Oh, Jesus."

Electric heat exploded in my core and rolled through the entire length of my body.

I let go of Kacey's cock and grabbed Tyler's head, holding on for dear life as he sucked each immense shudder of pleasure from my body.

"I'm so close," Kacey whined.

"Finish your fucking self, then," I replied raggedly as my body went limp and I collapsed against the mattress.

"Selfish."

"Distracted!"

He took a couple of shallow breaths. "Just as well. I don't want to miss out on the main event."

"I didn't think you would have a problem getting it up."

He arched an eyebrow at me. "Does it look like I have a problem?"

Biting my lip, I shook my head and watched as he hopped somewhat stiffly from the bed before returning my attention to Tyler. My gaze wandered down his lean body, stopping at the sight of a bead of moisture slipping from the slit of his swollen shaft.

"Just tell me this doesn't feel weird for you," he said as he climbed on top of me.

I reached down and wrapped my hand around his shaft, rubbing the drop of pre-cum into the bulbous head. His eyelids fluttered, Adam's apple bobbing as he gulped.

"I always thought…I thought it bad that I'd wondered about this so much, but no. It doesn't feel weird."

"I've wanted you for a very long time, Nikki."

I let go of him, pressed my hands into the mattress, and shifted backward. He followed me, and the sight sent a new wave of heat rolling over me, caused my core to tighten once more.

"And although I'm not helping my case at this very moment, it's not all about the sex for me."

"I know." I smiled sheepishly at him. "You're not Kacey."

"No, he's fucking not."

A condom packet landed next to my thigh, and my entire body clenched with anticipation. I reached for it, and the moment Tyler placed his hand on top of mine, I suddenly realized that I had started to shake slightly.

"We can stop."

"I don't want to." I pressed the packet to his hand. "I want to know what it would feel like to be with you. Both of you, just once." I lay back on the bed and opened my legs.

Tyler ripped the packet open, and swiftly, yet calmly, rolled the condom down his shaft. Leaning up, I kissed him tenderly as he moved over me and positioned himself between my thighs. His eyes locked on mine as he gripped my hips and slowly pushed inside me.

The air caught in my throat, making the sound of pleasure slipping past my lips broken and breathy. The friction felt amazing and I wanted to cry out as my channel stretched to fit him.

He whispered my name as he paused inside me, giving me a moment to adjust.

I slid my hands to his ass and pushed my hips upward, needing all of him.

"I never thought seeing you fuck someone would get me hard, but damn, how wrong was I?" Kacey commented raggedly.

A throaty laugh left Tyler's mouth as he pressed his forehead to mine. "I so hope that isn't directed at me, man."

"I honestly don't fucking know, but if your cock comes anywhere near me tonight, I will beat your ass."

"Trust me, my cock has no interest in you." A wicked grin slowly curled at the corner of Tyler's mouth as he ground his hips experimentally against mine. "Are you still with me?"

I looked up at him. "All the fucking way."

He withdrew so slowly that I wanted to cry at the feel of every inch of him slipping out of me. Just as I had been ready to protest over how empty I felt, he thrust back inside.

"Tyler, please."

He moved his hands to my hips as he withdrew again; only this time, he didn't pull so far. Instead, his hips fell into a beautiful rhythm that had me catching my breath each time he hit the perfect spot.

He looked down at me, and with shallow breath, whispered, "Are you all right?"

I dug my nails in to his ass and thrust my hips up to meet him in reply.

His eyelids fluttered shut and his head dropped to mine as he squeezed my hips. "Fuck, Nikki…."

"Real question is, are you ready for me, baby?"

My attention turned to the side of the bed where Kacey stood. His hand wrapped around his thick cock as he smeared a transparent liquid along the hard flesh. My gaze fell to the tube of K-Y jelly sitting on the bedside table, and nerves began to dance with the burning excitement in my gut.

Without warning, Tyler rolled onto his side, pulling me with him. I gulped as the bed dipped behind me. Tyler ran his right hand down my back and lifted my left leg, hooking it over his hip.

"We've got you," he said, leaning in and kissing my neck.

Kacey cupped my ass cheeks. He massaged my flesh in such a way that I wanted to purr. "Relax, baby girl."

I twisted to look at him. "I'm not exactly new to this."

A wide smile broke on his face. "You ain't gone boring, then."

"I told you I hadn't."

Tyler slid his hand down my stomach and slipped his finger between my wet folds. His finger encircled my clit as Kacey propped himself up on his elbow and kissed me. I tensed momentarily as Kacey slipped one lubed finger past the tight muscle of my anus. He kissed me slowly, nipping at my bottom lip while he rubbed the cool liquid in a lazy circle inside of me.

I jolted as Tyler pinched my clit. Our hips smashed together, the movement reminding me of why I currently felt so deliciously full.

Breaking the kiss, I groaned as I rubbed myself against and along Tyler. "Fuck me already. I can't take this much longer."

My whole body felt like a furnace. I could feel another orgasm curling deep inside and I desperately wanted to ride it.

Kacey grinned. "Don't have to beg me twice."

Tyler moved his hands to my ass and spread my cheeks as Kacey shifted into position behind me. Holding on to my hip, Kacey slowly pushed inside. I bit my lip and hissed as sharp pain seared through me.

Kacey groaned and eased himself in a little further. "Nearly there, baby."

My head fell to Tyler's shoulder, teeth sinking into his flesh as the sensation of being full to the point of splitting ran through me.

With a deep breath, Kacey tightened his grip on my waist and thrust inside me. I cried out at the double penetration, but the initial shock was short-lived as they began moving in unison. Kacey's hand wandered down my stomach as he took over the duty of stimulating my clit. Tyler took hold of my left breast and began massaging my nipple between his thumb and index finger.

Lifting my head, I glanced at Tyler. His face looked like a picture of ecstasy as he rocked into me. His slender lips parted as he breathed heavily. I wound my arm around him, my nails scorching his back as I closed my eyes and gave in to the feeling of being trapped between them.

A mixture of sweet and spicy cologne swirled round me as their heat cocooned my entire body. The mattress squeaked beneath us, providing the bass to a symphony of groans and slick sounds that quickly filled the motel room.

Kacey's mouth played along my nape and shoulder, his teeth nibbling my skin as he tortured my clit. Tyler's hand slid to my thigh, which he hiked higher on to his hip. We groaned together as his next thrust slid perfectly against my g-spot.

I felt so wet, and the ache deep inside pulsed so strongly, that I wanted to scream. Each sharp movement sent electricity shooting to my toes, and the feel of their hands gliding and clutching possessively at my body felt better than anything I had ever dreamed.

"I can't—oh, God I can't hold on much longer."

"Christ, I can feel you tightening," Kacey groaned into my ear. "Take us fucking with you, baby girl. Make us explode. Milk us dry."

I dropped my head to Tyler's shoulder as a mixture of intense pain and pleasure wrapped round me. I dug my nails into his back and moaned into his damp skin as their thrusts became more erratic. Each sharp hit pushed the ache inside higher and higher until I couldn't hold on any longer.

Their grips tightened as my body clamped down on them.

Liquid fire rolled through me like a hurricane, burning the cry of pleasure from my throat. My head swam, and the world twisted into a curtain of multicoloured stars on a sea of black. I felt Tyler tense, and through the dizzying haze of ecstasy, I could hear my name leaving his lips, quickly followed by a muffled curse from a rigid Kacey.

Lips skimmed the top of my hair as strong arms wrapped round my trembling, sedated body. Lifting my head, I looked at Tyler and smiled somewhat dreamily.

"That didn't feel weird," he said softly.

"No, it didn't."

"It felt pretty fucking hot, even if I do say so myself," Kacey exclaimed, rolling onto his back. "I'd never force you, baby girl, but I hope like hell you will consider replacing movie night with this."

I shook my head. "You're such a tool."

But damn, that idea was tempting.

"Yeah, and you just fucked me." He slapped my ass and rolled off the bed. "Clearly, you love me a whole lot more than you're letting on."

I bit my cheek and waited for the sting to subside, not really wanting to move from the warmth of Tyler's embrace. Once the bathroom door shut, I met his gaze. "Listen, I—"

"I never expected you to feel the same way about me," he said quietly. "I do love you, and maybe I should have told you ages ago, but you're my best friend before anything else and I didn't want that to change. I still don't. So if you wake up tomorrow and want to forget this amazing sex ever happened" —" He gave me a soft smile. "—that's fine."

I didn't feel awkward or weird, but I had no idea what I wanted to do. Sex was fun, and we trusted each other, so why couldn't this be something we shared on a regular basis?

The sound of running water met my ears, and I glanced over my shoulder toward the bathroom.

"I honestly don't think this is something that I will be able to forget," I said, looking back at Tyler. "I don't want to make promises to you, though, either of you. So let's just go with the flow?"

Untangling himself from me, he rolled off the bed. "Sounds good to me."

Following his lead, I climbed off the bed rather unsteadily and retrieved my clothes from the floor. I pulled my shorts on with difficulty and tapped my pocket to make sure my motel room key had stayed inside.

"Don't tell me you're thinking about running back next door?"

A grin curled on my mouth as I pulled my top over my head. "It would look a bit strange, wouldn't it? Jayne waking up and finding me gone and the door locked?"

He shrugged and walked over to the door, locking it. "Tell her you couldn't sleep."

"Yeah, like she's going to believe me—" I froze as a shadow wandered past the window. "Someone's outside."

Tyler moved across to the window and pulled the floral curtain back. He peeked round the thin fabric and shook his head. "No one's out there."

My stomach knotted as I moved next to him and took a look for myself. "But I saw someone walk past the window."

He laughed lightly. "Well, it is a motel, and there are other customers here."

"It's late, why would anyone—" I squeaked as he swept me off my feet and carried me back toward the bed.

"You really don't like motels, do you?" He dropped me on the bed and climbed up beside me. "No one's out there. I promise."

I handed him my room key to place on the bedside table. My gaze latched on to the window as I cuddled up to him. "Not now, but I did see someone."

"Well, no need to worry. You're safe with us," he stated as he pulled the covers over us and flicked the lamp off.

* * *

I have sat there long enough. Cramp has taken over my legs from being stuck in the confined space. The dark haired woman has left ages ago. Has shut the door, locked it. Will she be back? Or has she been kind enough to leave us alone?

I have been rock hard since they got back; since my redhead has stripped for me again. She has even put on something special for our first night together.

I will not keep her waiting any longer.

Pushing open the door, I slip into the room. I step carefully, so not to wake her. The others liked it when I have surprised them. My redhead will like it, too. She appears to be a heavy sleeper. Her snores have kept me company while I waited. The sound has soothed me in the dark.

Reaching out, I peel back the covers, stopping to admire the black silk she wears for me.

Thoughtful beauty. My sleeping beauty.

Chapter Four

Saturday 6th September 2014
9:58 a.m.

Waking up to see Kacey's smug face gave me one hell of a reality check. Not to mention a reminder of why there lingered a delicious ache between my thighs.

"For a girl who freaked out in all sorts of ways last night, you sure sleep well," he stated with a yawn.

I rubbed my eyes and rolled onto my back, glancing at the empty space beside me before propping myself up on my elbows, searching the room with sleep-filled eyes. The sunlight poured through the thin curtains, setting the room in a warm orange haze. The shuffle of feet and the sound of running water caught my attention and quickly clarified where Tyler had vanished to, meaning I lay alone in bed with Kacey. A giddy thrill skipped through me.

"What's that supposed to mean?"

"That you luckily missed the late night show that Shauna and Craig put on."

Heat licked my cheeks. "Shit, do you think they heard us?"

He arched his eyebrow. "Does it matter if they did?"

"Seems a bit shit of us after what happened between you two."

"What happened between Shauna and me was a

drunken mistake."

I snorted and flopped back in bed. "Yeah. A two-hour-long drunken mistake."

A predatory grin curved his lips, and he twisted on to his side. "Are you jealous?"

"Hardly."

Well, I had been, until last night.

My quick answer only caused him to laugh.

"Well, I came out of the bathroom to find you and Tyler half out of it last night. Otherwise—" He slid his hand over my stomach and pulled me on to my side. "—we could have gone for another round."

My entire body tightened as he pulled me against him. "Maybe next time."

"So there will be a next time?" He slipped his hand into my shorts and squeezed my ass.

A small moan caught in my throat. "Possibly."

Dipping his head to my nape, he kissed my pulse, sucking slowly on the sensitive flesh. "Because I have to be honest, Nikki. I'm a little jealous that Tyler got to taste and fuck you." He dragged my shorts over my hips. "It's a little unfair."

Heat pulsed in my core at the thought of being trapped under Kacey. He would fuck me harder than Tyler, and God, I wanted him to, but I couldn't do such a thing with Tyler in the other room.

"We can't." I pushed his hand away and adjusted my shorts.

"Why, because Ty isn't with us?"

"No. Because I need to go next door before Jayne wakes up, and you need to get your ass ready so we can get the hell out of here."

I pulled away from him and stumbled out of bed.

"Do you need me to say 'I love you'? Is that it?"

I turned and looked at him. "What?"

"You said you wanted me, but I feel like I got the short end of the deal." He propped his head on his hand. "So I want to know if the people who state that they're in love with you get the privilege of—"

I dropped my voice. "It's one thing for us all to agree to be with each other; it's another to have Tyler walk in here and see me fucking you. I'm not going to hurt him like that."

"I see." He rolled onto his back. "You don't mind hurting my feelings, though, do you, baby girl?"

I strangled a laugh. "Your feelings?"

"Yeah. Don't you think I felt hurt watching you both last night?"

Anger stabbed at me. I grabbed my room key off the nightstand.

"Honestly, no. I think you're just pissed because Tyler made his move first." I walked over to the door and unlocked it. "And you know what?" I opened the door and looked at him. "If you're going to be picky about what happened, then maybe it would be best if we did all just forget about it."

I slammed the door behind me and stared out at the field across the road. My jaw tensed. My temples throbbed. I forced myself to take a deep breath. Uncertainty and confusion swirled in my mind, but it quickly dispersed as I turned to find Sarah standing at the other end of the walkway. She wore a pale yellow sweater and a pair of faded jeans.

"Everything all right, dear?" she asked as she placed towels into her cleaning trolley.

I clutched my room key. "Fine, thank you."

"Did you sleep well?"

I walked toward my motel room door.

"Very well." With a forced smile, I quickly unlocked the door. "We're just getting ready and then we will be dropping the keys in."

"No rush." A smile claimed her face. "It's nice to have folks around. Get's lonely here sometimes."

"I imagine, but I'm afraid we have to hit the road soon."

"I understand. Well, when you're ready, I'll be waiting."

A chill claimed my back at the odd note of promise lying within her tone. Smile still in place, I slipped inside the room and shut the door, locking it quickly. I pressed my head to the wood, mentally preparing myself for the hard stare of a nosey redhead, but when I turned round, I found an empty bed.

"Jayne?"

No reply.

I walked over to the bathroom and pushed the door open only to find the small room empty. My unease began to twist further as I looked round the room. The dishevelled covers and pillows confirmed that I wasn't going crazy and that she had been in bed, but her case appeared to be missing. I pulled the door to the built-in wardrobe open, hoping like hell she was playing a childish prank to get back at me for my absence, but found it empty, and strangely cold.

A knock on the door caused my heart to flutter. "Who is it?"

"It's Shauna."

I walked over and unlocked the door, pulling it wide. "Is Jayne with you?"

Her brow furrowed. "Er, no. I actually came to see her."

"She's not here."

"Well, where is she?"

"I don't know." Guilt stabbed at me. "I, er—I kinda couldn't sleep so I went and had a few drinks and then crashed with Kacey and Tyler last night."

Shauna arched a perfectly plucked eyebrow. "You guys got wasted last night? You should have told us. We were so bored."

I shrugged. "We thought you two would want some 'alone time'."

She snorted. "Oh, heck, Craig's good, but he's not that good. Trust me. Getting wasted would have been a nice break."

I looked round the room. "I locked the door behind me, so how did she get out?"

Unease began to rapidly turn in my stomach.

"Maybe she climbed out of the window?" Shauna walked over to the window and pulled the curtains open —a single panel of glass had been welded to the frame. "Okay, maybe not."

My gut twisted. "Oh, God, what if something's happened to her? What if someone broke in and—"

"Nikki, be serious. You would know if someone had broken in. The window would be smashed, or the lock on the door would have been broken." She walked over to the bathroom doorway and glanced inside. "And your bathroom window is as small as ours is. So, no one got in."

"What if the lock was picked? What if—"

"Are you seriously suggesting that someone picked the lock, kidnapped Jayne, and then locked the door behind them? That's insane. Plus, ten minutes with her and they would have brought her straight back."

I wanted to find this ridiculous. I wanted to believe that Jayne had somehow gotten out and was playing a trick on me as payback, but my gut wasn't buying it. Something was very wrong.

"Jayne was locked inside this room. Tell me how the hell she got out?"

"I have no idea, but I'm sure there is a logical explanation."

She looked doubtful, and the sight made me all the more sick.

"Something's happened to her. I don't know what, but—" The steady humming of wheels caught my attention. I turned and looked at the window, watching as Sarah's shadow moved across the closed curtains. "I saw someone outside Kay and Ty's window last night. I don't know who it was. One of the other guests, or maybe the owners…and they have spare keys, don't they? Technically, they would be the only other people able to get into this room—"

Shauna appeared in front of me. She grabbed my arms and looked me dead in the eyes. "Nikki, you're talking crazy, and it's starting to freak me out. I don't know what happened, but let's not jump to conclusions.

There has to be a reasonable explanation for this."

She let go of my arms and glanced round the room once more as if there was some corner I had forgot to check. "Just get ready and go get Tyler and Kacey." A faint smile fluttered on her lips as she looked back at me. "Craig and I will go check at reception and ask the owners if they've seen her. Okay?"

I nodded. "Yeah, all right."

"Just relax. She could have gone for a walk or something," she stated before disappearing from sight.

Perhaps, but that still didn't explain how she got out of a locked room.

* * * * *

10:42 a.m.

I stared at the blinking message on my cell phone as it told me for the tenth time that I had no signal.

"You're getting yourself wound up for nothing," Tyler stated as I paced back and forth in his motel room.

"Look, I locked the door last night. I saw someone walk past the window, and then when I unlocked the door this morning, the room was empty."

"Listen to what you're saying. You unlocked the door," Kacey said. "Last time I checked, Jayne couldn't walk through walls."

"Besides, don't you think if someone had broken in, they would have smashed the window or busted the lock or something?" Tyler added.

"Shauna has already pointed that out, but don't forget, credit cards and pins can open a locked door. So can keys."

Tyler laughed. "What, you think the motel owner broke in and kidnapped Jayne?"

They had to have spare room keys, or a master key of some sort—meaning that they had access to every room in the building. So it was possible.

"Nikki." Kacey grabbed me by the shoulders. "You're talking crazy."

The door opened and Shauna and Craig walked in.

"Has Sarah seen her?" I shrugged off Kacey's hold.

"We've just been talking to Ernie?" Shauna looked at Craig. "That right?"

I nodded. "Yeah, she said that's her husband. What did he say?"

"He ain't seen no redhead," Craig mimicked.

I felt sick. "Well, someone has to have seen her, because we can't leave without her."

"This is fucking ridiculous." Kacey scrubbed his hands over his face.

"We better go and check with Sarah and ask her if we can use her phone and call Jayne off that," I said as I slipped my cell phone in to my jean pocket.

"What should we do?" Shauna asked, looking between us all.

"Search the area?" Kacey looked down at me. "What? We're in the middle of nowhere. Maybe she went sleep-walking and has passed out in a field."

"Firstly, she doesn't sleep-walk. Secondly, how did

she get out of the room?"

He shoved his hands in his pockets and shrugged. "I don't know."

"Then how can she be wandering around?"

"I was just making a suggestion, Nikki."

I took a deep breath. "I know. I'm sorry. I just…I want to find Jayne and get the hell out of here."

Moving around Shauna and Craig, I headed out the door.

"Look, we'll meet you back at the van in ten minutes," Tyler said as he and Kacey followed me out.

"Whatever you do, please don't leave me alone with Sarah," I begged quietly as we walked along the walkway. "I don't trust her."

Tyler's eyebrows collided. "Why?"

"I just get a horrible feeling when I'm around her, that's all."

"Trust me." Kacey bumped his elbow with mine. "We ain't letting you out of our sight."

We watched as Sarah emerged from the first motel room. Locking the door, she turned and faced us. A wide smile spread on her face. "Are you leaving, dears?"

"Not yet." Kacey gave her a friendly smile. "You haven't seen a redhead, by any chance? She's very thin and quite short. She wears big heels, a lot of make-up, and has bright red nails. She's very hard to miss."

Sarah cocked her head slightly. "No, I'm afraid I haven't seen any girls that fit that description."

My jaw tensed. "Have you seen any girls at all?"

"Just you." Her glacial gaze turned to me, her cool

eyes sweeping from my head to my feet in a severe evaluation. "Oh, and that young lady over there." She glanced round me and her expression sharpened.

I turned to see Shauna and Craig walking around the corner of the motel, disappearing from sight.

"In fact, I've only seen you two," she said, looking between me and Kacey. "And now, we have another handsome gentleman also." Her focus moved to Tyler and her smile turned bright.

"Could we possibly use your phone?" Tyler asked politely.

Her brow furrowed as if he had just asked her something stupid. "Whatever for?"

"Well, our cell phones haven't got any reception," I explained, fighting to keep my own smile from turning hostile. "We think we might have more luck if we rang Jayne's cell phone off a land line."

Understanding crossed the woman's face, followed by a glint of amusement. "If your cell phones haven't got reception, will hers?"

My spine went rigid as the distinct feeling of ice clawed down my back. I stared at her for a moment and wondered if she had deliberately tried to brush the matter aside by making us appear crazy, or perhaps she was just plain dumb. "It's worth a shot, right?"

"I guess so." Her smile remained sharp. "Come with me, then, and I will take you into the office."

"Thank you." I waited for Sarah to turn her back and walk ahead of us before looking at Tyler and Kacey. "Still think I'm being paranoid?"

"Okay, she's a little weird. I admit it," Kacey replied. "And the way she looked at Shauna and Craig, what's that about?"

"Maybe she doesn't like people sneaking around her property," Tyler replied. "That's understandable."

"Jayne's missing," I growled at him.

"I know."

"Then start acting like you give a shit," I snapped, before making my way over to the entrance.

I stepped inside the reception and looked at Sarah, holding the top of the counter up.

"I'm afraid the office is rather snug, dear. So only you can go in."

"That's fine. We'll just wait here," Kacey said, coming through the door after me.

My feet felt like lead as I forced myself to walk toward the counter. I shimmied through the medium gap and waited for Sarah to lead me into the office. Tall book shelves lined two of the four walls, each shelf packed to the brim. Unease fluttered through me at the sight of three shotguns sitting neatly on an antique display rack on one of the empty walls.

Sarah must have noticed me staring because she chuckled at my sudden hesitation to move any farther into the room.

"Those have been in Ernie's family for years. Just a little something that belonged to his great-grandfather. Useless antiques."

I could do nothing but nod.

"Well, help yourself." Sarah pointed to the white hunk of plastic which sat on top of the large desk in the centre of the room.

I was surprised to see a modern computer in the

establishment, since the guestroom televisions looked like they belonged in the eighties.

"Thanks." I slid my cell phone from my pocket and scrolled to Jayne's number in my phone book.

"I do hope your friend hasn't gotten herself lost." Sarah took a seat on the chair in front of me. "It's so easily done round these parts."

I wanted her to be right. I really hoped that something as stupid and as innocent as getting lost was the reason, but…"I highly doubt it. She was locked in the room. So, logically, she should have been there when I went back inside."

I watched carefully as her expression flattened.

"I hope she didn't use anything to break the door handle. I'd have to charge you for that."

"Why would she?"

She cocked her head to the side. "She had to get out of the room somehow, didn't she, dear?"

"Yeah, and I assure you she didn't break the lock to do so," I replied sharply before dialling Jayne's number. Refusing to meet her gaze, I placed the phone to my ear. Silence met me, before the phone cut off. My stomach turned. Jayne never had her phone off. Maybe the battery had died. Perhaps she didn't have any signal. Perhaps she didn't have her cell phone…Shit.

I risked a glance at Sarah, happy to see her focus locked on the computer screen and not me. I kept the phone at my ear and watched as her jaw tightened and she shifted in her seat. My anxiety turned to sudden curiosity.

"Will you just excuse me for a moment, dear?" She leant forward and turned the monitor off. "I forgot I have a pie in the oven for lunch."

Standing, she quickly wandered through the inner office door on the left, shutting it behind her.

I placed the phone on the receiver and moved round the desk, pushed the power button to the monitor on, and wiggled the mouse. The screen blinked to life, and to my surprise, it filled with four colourful squares of the motel.

In the top left square, I saw Tyler and Kacey talking, their focus fixed to the office door, waiting. The top right square showed the full length of the empty parking lot. Bottom left, I caught sight of Shauna and Craig wandering round the back of the motel.

My gaze fell to the bottom right square, and my brow furrowed. It appeared to be one of the guest bedrooms. I stared at the square, watching with confusion as a man with long, dark hair paced the length of the floor. Every couple of seconds, he would lift his arms and gesture in a way that suggested he was talking to someone in the empty room.

My heart froze as he turned and Jayne's red suitcase came in to view.

"Oh, shit." Why did he have Jayne's case? Was she with him? Was she all right?

The screen blinked, filling with another four squares, and my gut went cold as I realized that cameras had been placed in the guest rooms. All of the rooms.

They'd been watching us. They'd been watching since we arrived.

My stomach churned at the thought and I suddenly felt as though bugs crawled beneath my skin.

They had seen everything.

Pins and needles stabbed at me. My head felt light, and I suddenly couldn't breathe.

Footsteps caught my attention.

With shaking hands, I quickly turned the monitor off and made my way to the front of the desk. Checking I hadn't knocked anything over, I placed my hand on the receiver as Sarah stepped back in to the room.

She shut the door and made her way round the desk. "No luck?"

"Unfortunately not." I folded my arms. "It was worth a shot, though."

She stopped in front of the computer, her focus dropping to the black screen. "Maybe you should head into town? Clearly, she found some way out of the room and has no doubt gone wandering to let off a little steam."

I dug my nails in to my arms, wanting desperately to scratch away the dirt that felt like it clung to me. "A little steam?"

A smile spread on her lips. "Personally, I'd be pissed if my friend had locked me in a room and left me alone."

Every inch of my skin crawled. I felt exposed under her heavy gaze, and the thought that she and her husband had footage of Tyler, Kacey and me… I wanted to be sick, but more to the point, I wanted to get the hell out of there. "No, I think it might be best if we just stayed here and waited for her to come back."

Sarah shook her head. "You could be waiting all day. It's a long way into town from here."

I forced a small smile. "That's fine. We're in no rush."

I turned and grabbed the handle to the door, pushing with more force than intended. My legs felt as though they were trembling with each step I took back in to the reception.

I stared at Kacey and Tyler with wide eyes while moving through the hatch in the counter. They exchanged a puzzled look.

Sarah followed me out. "So, you will be hanging on to your keys?"

"I think it would be best, yes."

"All right then, dears." She smiled. "If you decide you're staying another night, though—"

"We'll let you know," I said as I stopped in the doorway and my gaze moved across the two cars sitting in the parking lot. "Have any of your other guests signed out yet? It would probably be a good idea if we ask them if they've seen Jayne."

Sarah's brow furrowed. "What other guests?"

I indicated to the cars in the lot. My mind filled with the sight of dull lights leaking through the windows of three bedrooms as we pulled in the night before.

"Oh, child, they're our cars." She laughed lightly. "You kids are the only guests at the motel."

Dread filled me. "I see. Never mind, then."

I left the reception as calmly as I could.

Who was that man? Who had been in the rooms? Why weren't the cars outside the reception or round the back? Had they purposely been put there to make it look like the motel had customers? Had certain rooms been lit so it looked like people stayed in this isolated place?

Knots of sickness developed in my stomach with each unsteady step I took across the lot. My chest grew tight. My head felt light and I didn't know if it had something to do with lack of food or maybe because everything I could see around me looked wrong, like a big fat lie.

"Would you care to explain what is going on?" Kacey asked, hot on my tail.

I walked all the way to the back of his van and out of Sarah's sight. "She's lying."

I pressed my back to the warm metal.

"About what?" Tyler asked.

I placed my hands on my stomach and took a deep, steadying breath. "There's someone else here. I saw a man on their CCTV."

"What? Wait a minute." Kacey looked at me. "Did you call Jayne?"

"I tried Jayne's number but her phone just cut off. Sarah left me in the office for a couple of minutes. Made some excuse after she had looked at the computer. For some reason, I was curious. She looked really pissed. So, I took a look myself and there are CCTV cameras everywhere."

Tyler shrugged. "So? A lot of strangers pass through here. It's a normal safety precaution."

I stared at him, hating how calm he could be over everything. "Is it normal to have cameras in every single one of the guest bedrooms?"

Shock claimed his features, and his cheeks flushed slightly.

Kacey's expression hardened. "Those dirty fucking bastards."

I grabbed his arm before he went storming off into the reception. "As much as I feel sick at the thought of someone watching us, I'm more concerned about the fact that there is a man pacing backward and forward in one of the bedrooms, and he has Jayne's suitcase."

"Are you sure it's Jayne's?" Kacey asked through clenched teeth.

"Yes." I let go of his arm and looked between them both. "I think they've done something to Jayne."

"Like what?"

"I don't know, Ty. What if they've hurt her, or, God forbid, killed her or something?"

Tyler sighed. "Nikki, we get that you're worried, but what you're suggesting—"

"Don't!" I pointed at him. "Don't you dare try and make out like I am being irrational. Don't look at me like I'm being paranoid! I am telling you there is a man in this motel and he has Jayne's case in his room. Somehow, he must have gotten a key and—"

"Hey." Kacey placed his hand on my shoulder. "Take a deep breath. We're jumping to conclusions here. Jayne could be fine. She could be walking her hangover off."

I wanted to believe that. God, I wanted her to walk round the corner so we could strangle her for taking off, and then just get the hell out of there.

"How long are we going to keep saying that? Another hour? Are we going to wait here all day, hoping? Why is it so hard to believe that something could have happened to her? We're in the middle of freaking nowhere and these people are weird. I mean, why is Sarah lying about other people being at the motel? Why does that man have Jayne's suitcase? How did she disappear from a locked room? Why aren't they even trying to help us find Jayne? Instead, they're eager to see us on our way."

"All right." Tyler placed his hands on his hips. "I think it's time we call the police."

"Fuck, yeah." Kacey pulled away from me. "Get these perverts arrested for invasion of privacy."

"I want to believe that Jayne is fine, but we can't call the police until we know for sure where she is." I wiped at my cheeks. "One of those cameras will have recorded what happened to her. We need to check the CCTV footage for last night."

Tyler ran his hand through his hair and took a deep breath. "Okay, but how are we going to do that? I doubt these two are going to let us snoop round their office."

"There are five of us and two of them," I replied, waving Shauna and Craig over as they walked across the lot. "Surely, we can think of something?"

* * *

"You stupid, stupid boy. How many times I got to tell you to drug 'em and leave 'em where you found 'em?"

I cry out as the leather belt hits my bare back once again. My skin burns after each whack. It hurts. It always hurts.

She gets upset when I play with the guests a little too much. She doesn't like when they won't wake up. She doesn't like when I move them.

"I don't trust these kids, Sarah." He stands near the

window watching my redhead's friends as they talk. "They're up to something. Kids are always up to something."

"Well, their friend is missing and they're worried about her." She walks over to the bathroom door. Disgust washes over her features as she stares inside the small room. "They are set on finding her, which means they will stick around, and whose fault would that be?"

I dig my nails into my skin and hug my thighs tighter, waiting for the next hit.

"How many times do I have to tell you, George? Only go for the ones that are single, or in pairs. And at least leave 'em with a pulse when you're finished playing with them. Now, we got ourselves a litter of nosey little kittens snooping round. I'm sick of cleaning up your mess, boy." She walks back over to me. Grabbing a fistful of my hair, she yanks my head back and presses her nose to mine. "I ought' a put you down like the dumb dog you are."

I whimper as pain slices through my skull.

"Leave him be. Boy don't know any better, and you know it."

"He's sloppy. We should put him on a damn leash. Teach him a lesson."

"Ain't his fault no one comes through here."

"Yeah, but it's his fault we're stuck here." She lets go of my head and straightens. "It's his fault for getting excited, and forgetful."

I scurry into the corner the moment she turns her back and walks over to the window. "Where are they going?"

He shakes his head. "Ain't got a clue. Maybe they

are heading in to town to look for her."

"No. That girl said the door was locked. She knows something ain't right."

"Well, then, I don't know where those three are off to, but the other two have headed into the reception."

"These kids are getting on my last nerve, Ernie. I want 'em gone."

"I guess we better get in there, then, and give them one last chance to hit the road." He walks over to the door and opens it.

"You better be quiet boy, you understand?"

I bob my head, not stopping until the door has shut and the lock has slid into place.

Chapter Five

12:26 p.m.

We watched from the field across the road as Shauna and Craig coaxed Sarah and her dumpy, sandy-haired husband, Ernie, round the back of the motel to the field where they'd 'found something.'

The plan seemed shit, but we didn't exactly have much to work with. The impression the motel owners had was that we three had gone off searching the area in case Jayne had 'gotten herself lost.' We just needed ten minutes to get into the office and check last night's footage.

The moment we saw the four of them disappear round the building, we ran across the lot as quickly and quietly as possible. My heart beat so loudly, I felt as though everyone could hear it and would come running. Naturally, they didn't.

Side by side, we pressed our backs against the stone wall.

"All right, there's a camera in the reception and one looking out into the lot, but quite frankly, I couldn't give a damn if they see we've been sneaking. I just want to find Jayne and get out of here."

"Let's do this, then." Kacey slipped round the corner and through the open doorway of the reception.

Tyler and I followed.

"Jesus, it is small in here," Kacey commented as he stepped inside the office.

I walked straight to the desk and switched the monitor on. Taking a seat, I watched as the grid of four images appeared before me, each one a motel room, the cameras positioned so that the bed and door to the bathroom could be viewed.

A shudder rocked me at the thought of the motel owners watching the three of us; at their eyes burning into our skin as they watched every caress and every movement. My stomach turned.

The screen flickered to the next four images and the dishevelled bedding of mine and Jayne's room caught my eye. I clicked on the image, hoping it would make it bigger, but nothing. "Shit."

"What?" Tyler moved next to me.

"I don't know how to make the image bigger."

"Here." He crouched down and clicked a few buttons. The image of our room filled the screen. The camera rendition turned into different hues of green. "Night vision."

"I guessed."

Moving the mouse to the bottom of the page, he dragged the slider across the bar. At four minutes past three, I watched myself get out of bed and sneak across the room until I was off camera. Guilt churned in my gut as I stared at Jayne, fast asleep and right where I left her.

"Is there any way to move it forward slowly?"

Tyler swiftly tapped a few buttons, and the time began to jump forward two minutes at a time. At four-thirty, movement in the bottom left-hand corner of the screen caught my eye, and horror flooded me as the wardrobe door opened and the dark-haired man from the footage I saw earlier crawled through the doorway and made his way toward Jayne.

"Oh, shit," Tyler muttered. "How the fuck—?"

"What?" Kacey moved to my other side and his eyes widened. "Is that the same guy you saw earlier?"

I nodded. Dread filled me from head to foot and no matter how hard I tried to look away, I couldn't pull my focus from the image before me. The man deftly moved the cover from Jayne and pushed her chemise up, before shoving his dark jogging pants down. Thick waves of bile coated my entire mouth, and I dug my nails in to my knees.

I watched in horror as Jayne stirred, as her hands flew up to the male's face. As he covered her mouth with his hand and forced her legs apart with the other. My entire body clenched as he moved on top of her.

My stomach retched and acid heat crawled up my throat. I gagged.

"Don't, baby girl." Kacey placed his hand on my back. "Not here."

Tyler grabbed the mouse and moved the slider fifteen minutes later, stopping when the man moved off Jayne. He pulled his pants up as if everything was normal, then he tilted his head to the side. Leaning down, he clutched her shoulders and shook her vigorously. Glancing toward the door, he shook her again until Jayne's head fell limply to the side.

"Oh, God, I knew it. I knew something was wrong." I choked as tears swelled in my eyes. "Oh, God, she's dead. They've fucking killed her."

"No." Tyler shook his head and continued to move the slider along the bar. "No, that doesn't make sense. She can't be, not like that. She just can't."

We watched as the man wandered round the room. His head kept swinging back to Jayne as if expecting her to snap out of it. When she didn't move, he would hit his head with the palm of his hand.

Tyler continued to drag the slider slowly over the bar at the bottom of the screen. Finally, after fifteen minutes had passed, the man grabbed Jayne's ankles and pulled her off the bed. He dragged her along the floor like she was a ragdoll, pulling her over to the wardrobe until he disappeared inside.

"What the fuck is he doing?" Kacey asked through clenched teeth.

The man stretched out of the wardrobe, his hands encircling her legs as he pulled her downward.

"There's a hidden door in the wardrobe." I hiccupped. "That has to be it. How…how else is he doing that?"

A moment later, the man crawled out and wiggled across the floor to collect her suitcase.

"Computer whiz, can you get a copy of that for the cops?" Kacey looked at Tyler, who just nodded.

I stood up and walked to the opposite wall. My shoulder hit the brick and I stared at the tarnished wooden floor. "Jayne's dead. She's dead and it's all my fault. I should have stayed with her. I should have—"

"What, so that sick bastard could have done the same to you? No fucking way." Kacey turned to the shelves and began moving items aside.

Tears swelled in my eyes as I shook my head idly.

"Jayne's dead because of me. I locked her in the room. I left her alone. I shouldn't have left her alone."

"No, she's dead because some fucking pervert broke into the room and killed her."

And maybe if I had stayed with her, I could have fought him off; we both could have. Maybe if I'd been there, Jayne would have had a chance. She might still be alive.

"Thank fuck for that." Kacey grabbed hold of a disc from one of the shelves and passed it to Tyler. "Use this."

"Why wouldn't they have called the cops?" Tyler slid the disc into the machine. "It wasn't Ernie. That guy looked thinner, taller, and a lot younger."

"They had to know. How else did he know about a secret entrance into that room?" I looked at Kacey. "He has to be with them. Why else would she lie about him being here?" My stomach retched again. "Why are they doing this? Why is there another way into that room?"

"Only one reason I can think of, and I didn't think people did shit like this." Tyler's eyes darted over the screen. "Record strangers and sell their private moments."

I pressed my back against the wall and took a deep breath. "Like people having sex?"

"Sex, or violence. There are twisted people out there who would pay for shit like that."

"Even watching a murder?"

"Possibly."

A sob caught in my throat. "Oh, God."

"We need to get out of here," Kacey stated. "We need

to get Shauna and Craig and just get the fuck out of here, right now."

"What about Jayne?"

"She's dead, baby girl. There's not much we can do for her."

"How can we know for sure? Maybe she passed out. We can't just leave her here. Lord knows what they'll do to her."

Kacey walked over to me and cupped my face. "We take this disc and we go to the cops. Fucking city cops. We got proof. We can come back with them and we'll find Jayne, but right now, we have to—"

Kacey's head swung to the office door as distinct gunfire sounded, quickly followed by a shrill scream.

"Oh, shit." I shifted away from the wall. "Oh, shit, did they just—"

I looked up at the shotgun rack to find two of the guns missing. "Useless antiques, my ass."

"Ty, you finished with that disc?" Kacey asked as he reached up and grabbed the remaining shotgun from the rack. "We kinda need to get out of here."

"Almost," Tyler said as he drummed his fingers across the keys. "Fuck."

"What?" I moved round the desk beside him and watched the footage on the computer monitor. My eyes widened at the sight of Ernie dragging a struggling Shauna across the car lot. "Oh, God, what's he going to do to her?"

"Hurry, Ty." Kacey pushed me to one side and pulled open the desk drawers. "Now we're fucking talking." He turned and grabbed my hand. "You take this—" He placed a letter opener in my palm. "—and you get into their apartment."

"What?" I shook my head. "No. I'm not taking this. I'm not going in there."

"I'm afraid you have to, baby." He pulled open another drawer and continued searching.

"What are you fucking looking for?"

"Shells."

"What? Are you fucking crazy? You don't even know how to use a gun."

"Sure, I do." His face lit up as he pulled open the bottom drawer. He pulled out a box filled with thick red tubes topped with gold. "I just point at the psychopaths, pull the trigger, and hope to God I hit them in a fucking good place."

"Kacey—"

"Nikki, they have guns. Do you want me to be Captain Obvious and state that we are in one seriously fucked up situation right now?" He flipped the barrel down and slid seven shells inside. "That not taking something to protect ourselves with would be a dumb fucking idea?"

My jaw trembled. "I—I'm scared. Kay, I'm really fucking scared."

Clicking the barrel back into place, he looked at me.

"I know, baby. You're not the only one." He retrieved his keys from his pocket and shoved them in mine. "The first chance you get, climb out of a window, and once the coast is clear, you get to my van and you get the engine running."

"I'm not leaving you both here."

"Done." Tyler slid the disc from the machine. His

dark eyes didn't move from the screen. "He's dragging Shauna into one of the rooms."

"Who the hell said anything about leaving us?" Kacey smiled crookedly as he cupped my face with his right hand. "I'm sorry for being an ass earlier, or rather in general, all right?"

I shook my head. "Forget earlier."

"I care about you a lot, Nicole. I just know that I'm not right for you in the ways you need, and I hate it."

I placed my hand on top of his. "Kacey—"

"I'm sorry I dragged you all on this stupid trip. Whatever has happened to Jayne is my fault, not yours, but we're gonna get out of here, okay?"

"How?"

"No idea, but you just gotta trust me? I'm not gonna let anything happen to you. To either of you."

"I do trust you." I leant in and kissed him with trembling lips. "Please don't do anything stupid."

He laughed faintly. "I'll try."

Tyler stood up and shoved the disc in his back pocket. "Okay, we need to go."

He moved past us and carefully opened the inner office door.

"Go on, baby," Kacey said as he pulled away.

I turned and followed Tyler through the open doorway. The sound of Sarah's and Ernie's voices grew louder as they entered the reception, and my heart jumped into my throat. Kacey shut the door quietly behind us and we moved swiftly along the short hallway and into a living room.

The white wallpaper with large pink roses in bloom

matched the dusky pink curtains and somewhat worn sofa and chairs. A fairly modest living room with sun leaking through two medium-sized windows on the facing wall made it almost easy to feel safe.

"The windows," Tyler whispered.

We all ran to the same window, our hands sliding across the glass and along the frame. Tears continued to crawl down my cheeks, their presence fogging up my sight.

"There's no latch." I choked and backed away.

A tense Kacey passed the shotgun to Tyler before he moved round the furniture and headed to the door on the left. Tyler and I shuffled past the sofa and watched as he pushed the door open and walked into the bedroom. He headed for the first window and growled. "No fucking latch."

The office door slammed shut, and I froze and slowly turned my head to the left. My gaze wandered down the small hallway, fixing on to the wooden door. My grip on the letter opener tightened.

"What I wanna' know is where the other three are," Sarah commented bitterly.

"I don't think they'll have gone too far, darlin'." Ernie's rough drawl vibrated through the walls. "But if they stay another night, we might be able to get another show off 'em."

"I better check the cameras. I don't trust 'em, especially that girl."

My stomach clenched as another wave of sickness rolled over me. I looked at Kacey.

"Go," he mouthed.

My jaw trembled as I shook my head. Tyler grabbed

my free hand and pulled me into the kitchen. My legs felt as though they would give way any minute.

"We can't leave him," I whispered as he moved toward the back door.

"We need to get out of here and get to the van." He twisted the handle. "If we can draw them outside, then Kay can get out."

The lock slid out of place and the door creaked open.

"Where in God's name is my great-granddaddy's shotgun?" Ernie boomed.

"They've been in 'ere," Sarah shrieked. "Those little bastards have been in 'ere."

Ice claimed my veins as I looked at Kacey. The expression on his face as he looked through the private apartment at us mirrored the agony twisting in my heart.

Fear wrapped around my throat tightly, squeezing his name from me. "Kacey."

He closed the bedroom door, shutting himself in.

A loud bang echoed in the living room. Tyler grabbed my arm and pulled me through the door just as Sarah rounded the corner.

Stumbling backward, I twisted and began to run with Tyler down the back of the motel. The L-shaped building seemed so long as a blur of light stone and dark windows merged together in the corner of my eye. My heart thundered in my chest as I heard the back door hit the wall.

"You little bastards," Ernie thundered.

I threw a look over my shoulder and my eyes widened at the sight of Ernie lifting a shotgun in our direction. "Tyler, duck."

We both stumbled. Our knees hit the dirt as gunfire echoed in the space around us. Dull pain licked at my legs and the letter opener slipped from my hand as I tried to cushion my fall.

"Are you okay?"

I nodded and quickly scrambled to my feet. We rounded the corner of the building. My focus locked onto Kacey's camper van and adrenaline burst through me as I picked up pace and sprinted across the lot. We were going to be okay. We were going to get out of here.

Then the bullet hit me.

Burning pain exploded in my right thigh, quickly consuming all other senses. I tried to move my leg, but the next thing I knew; the ground had risen up to meet me. My head hit the dirt, the grains rough against my skin as a pain, sharp and sudden, raced through my head.

The world around me bled black as my mind filled with a dream-like fog.

I was vaguely aware that Tyler had screamed my name.

I flinched as the loud pop of gunfire echoed in my ears once, twice, three times.

"Ernie!" Sarah's voice sliced through me, the high-pitch scream piercing my temples.

Another round went off. Someone hit the ground.

I groaned as hands clutched at me and hoisted me up. I turned over and squinted when light hit my face and stung my eyes.

"Nikki?" Tyler's voice came fast and breathless. "Shit, you're bleeding."

His hand moved over my thigh and I cried out as hot needles stabbed at me.

"Shit."

I forced my eyes open and Tyler's blurry face came in to view. "What happened?"

"She shot you." He pulled his T-shirt over his head. "So I shot her."

I blinked. "Where's—where's Ernie?"

"I…I think I killed him. It all happened so fucking fast. I saw you go down and I just turned and aimed, and—"

"Why couldn't you have just left?" Sarah screeched.

I turned my head to find her lying on the ground. Blood oozed from a gaping hole in her left thigh. "We wanted to find our friend. We know that man killed her. We saw—"

"My baby didn't mean to kill that little slut," she replied with a clenched jaw as she pushed herself onto her elbows. "He gets a little excited sometimes, forgets that he needs to give 'em a little something so they don't fight."

"He raped her." I cried out as Tyler wrapped his T-shirt tightly around my thigh.

"What do you care?" She reached for her shotgun. "You swan off to go spread your legs for these pretty boys."

Tyler lifted the gun and shot the ground near her feet. She flinched.

"Don't even think about it."

A vicious smile emerged on her face as her glacial gaze locked on to him. "You really think she's going to give a damn about you, boy? Girl that can drop her panties for any man ain't the type of girl you want to be takin' home to your mamma."

"And I suppose you're ideal, huh?" He lifted my arm and placed it round his neck. "Placing cameras in motels and letting your son molest and murder innocent strangers, and then selling it? You're worse than the people who watch this shit. You're sick."

Blistering pain shot through me as he threaded his arm round my waist and carefully pulled me up with him.

"Sick?" Sarah laughed. "No, sick is when a doctor tells a mother that her son is wrong. Sick is when they take him away from her and pump him full of all sorts of drugs. Sick is making a man who is just different—special—worse and then take all his parents' money to try and get him better."

She pushed her hand in to the dirt and began dragging herself backward. "Sick is chargin' us all our life savings just so we can have him home."

"What, and locking him up in a room, letting him rape people, is fine?" I asked through clenched teeth.

"He has the run of the whole motel," she said defensively. "We keep an eye on him. That's what the cameras were for, but after the first unfortunate event—" She shrugged. "—we figured we could make a bit of money."

My heart fluttered as Kacey appeared in the doorway of the reception. He raised his finger to his lips and began tiptoeing toward Sarah.

"You're a sick old bitch," I told her.

"Say what you want. We got to make ends meet somehow. No one comes through here anymore, and we can go weeks, maybe even months, without seeing anyone. Times are hard and it's lonely out here. My George gets excited when he hears a commotion. Your little whore made his night."

"And this is going to make my entire fucking weekend."

Sarah snapped her head round as Kacey stopped beside her. A crooked smile claimed his face as he lifted a large floral vase and smashed it over her head. She flopped on the ground.

He walked over to us. "I thought I told you to get out of here." His focus dropped to my leg. "Shit, Nikki. Are you okay?"

As soon as he came close enough, I slapped him across the face. "And I thought I told you to not do anything stupid."

He blinked and rubbed at his cheek.

"Stupidity is a hard habit to break." He threaded his arm around my waist and took me from Tyler's hold. "And just for the record, I'm against hitting women."

"Yeah, and I'm against shooting them," Tyler added as he walked over and picked up Sarah's shotgun.

"What happened to Papa Perv?" Kacey asked, taking both of the shotguns from him. "He dead?"

"Not sure," Tyler said before jogging to where Ernie lay.

Kacey's lips brushed against my temples. "Do I get a blow job for knocking the bitch out?"

I closed my eyes and took a steadying breath. "That depends. Did you call the cops during your game of hide and seek?"

"The moment I saw you idiots standing here having a conversation . . . you bet your fine ass I called them."

Relief flooded me. "Then yeah, I think you deserve a blow job."

"Just had to go through Hell, and nearly die, to decide that, did you?"

He chuckled as I punched him in the ribs. Opening my eyes, I looked over at Tyler. He kicked Ernie; the motel owner wobbled. "Shit."

"Nice going," Kacey called.

My gaze snagged on the red motel room doors, and my eyes widened. "Oh, God, Shauna."

I slipped from his arms and began limping as quickly as I could; trying my best to ignore the sharp pain that pulsed in my thigh with every unsteady step I took. "Which room did he put her in?"

Tyler grabbed Ernie's shotgun from the ground. "I don't know."

"Hey?"

I looked over at Kacey. He threw one of the shotguns to me.

"Just point and shoot, baby girl."

With a nod, I watched as Kacey ran over to the first guest room and shot the lock. The door creaked open. He pushed at the wood with the barrel of the gun and looked inside. "Empty."

My attention swung to Tyler as he shot door number fourteen and pushed it open. "Likewise."

I stumbled to door number seven and shot twice at the lock. The door opened, and I carefully pushed it open. "Also empty."

I moved to door eight and did the same. The gun popped. Empty. "Damn it."

I moved to the door and hit the wood with the butt of the gun and froze as the door opened slightly. Pushing the wood, I stepped into the room and placed the empty gun against the wall. My gaze dropped to the jeans discarded on the floor. I hobbled over to the bed where Shauna lay and my chest clenched at the sight of her. Blood stained her forehead, and her cheeks looked swollen. I threw the covers over her body and fell on the bed beside her placing my finger on her pulse. My gaze slipped down to the bruises wrapped around her throat and I realized why she didn't move.

"Oh, God, Shauna, I'm so sorry. I'm so, so—"

My head snapped round as the wardrobe door sprung open. I screamed as George ran out of the wardrobe and dived at me, his hazel eyes bloodshot and frantic as he landed on me like a ton weight. Words spilled from his narrow lips in a flurry but their meaning was lost due to the beat of my heart hammering in my ears. Panic swelled within my chest as I struggled to fight him off.

He grabbed my thighs and I cried out as the pressure of his large hands on my bullet wound sent heat spiralling up my spine. He pulled, his hands quickly sliding down my legs and claiming my ankles as he moved swiftly toward the wardrobe.

"Kacey!" I grabbed hold of the bedding, panicking when the sheets began to slip. "Tyler!"

Tears streamed from my eyes, and my sobs choked

me as the bedding hit the floor. I twisted and tried to grab a hold of something, but found nothing.

Kacey came through the doorway first. He held his shotgun firmly, but at the sight of George, he froze. "Fuck."

I looked down in time to see him dropping into a hole at the bottom of the wardrobe. "Oh, God."

Kacey fell to the floor. He dropped his gun and grabbed my arms. "Tyler!"

Tyler appeared in the doorway, only to disappear again.

George tightened his grip on my legs and pulled. My knees slipped through the hole. The burning in my leg pulsed through me as the edge of the wooden floor pressed into the backs of my thighs.

"Don't let go of me." I shook my head side to side. "Please, Kacey. Don't let go."

"Never, baby. I got you."

I dug my nails into his arms as he tightened his grip and pulled. Pain spiralled around my body from my toes to my head, and fear had me shaking. I watched my blood soak through my jeans and Tyler's T-shirt as I moved my legs as much as possible, hoping that George's grip would loosen any minute so I could kick him, but it didn't. He kept my legs pinned together. He squeezed my ankles in his iron grip and continued to pull.

Gunfire echoed round us.

"Get the fuck off her," Tyler demanded.

Another shot, and then another, again and again, until finally, George's grip went slack.

I kicked, frantically trying to push myself along the floor.

Kacey slid his hands to my waist and dragged. My legs slipped out of the hole, and hysterical laughter bubbled in my throat. Kacey pulled me into his embrace, locking me in his arms. His chest rose and fell heavily as I melted against him. I felt his hot breath against my skin as he pressed a kiss to my head.

"Tyler?"

"I'm good." A shotgun rose out of the hole, followed by Tyler. "It's fucking dark down there."

"Is he—he dead?"

"Well, if he ain't, he's going to be in a shit lot of pain, put it that way."

I grabbed the gun and slid it out the way before I reached for him. He climbed on top of me and collapsed. "Is Shauna—"

"Yeah."

"I found Jayne," Kacey commented raggedly. "She's in the shower stall in room one."

"Is she definitely—" Words caught in my throat.

He tightened his grip on me. "I'm sorry, baby."

"I think Craig might be, as well," Tyler said breathlessly. "I think he's round the back. Everything happened so quickly. I can't be sure."

I opened my mouth only to close it again. I didn't know what to say. I didn't even know what to think. In less than twenty-four hours, three of our friends had died….

"Oh, God, what—why—" My voice cracked as a sob wedged in my throat.

I turned and buried my face in to Kacey's shoulder as tears spilled down my cheeks. I clutched at Tyler, pulling him to me as shock overtook me and my entire body began to tremble.

Kacey pressed his face in to my hair. "We've got you."

Tyler pressed his forehead to my arm and kissed my skin. "It's all over."

Chapter Six

15:38 pm

Sirens had rung in the distance as the three of us lay huddled on the floor, and as the sound grew louder, along with the crunch of tires across gravel, I knew we were finally safe.

With Tyler's help, I managed to get to my feet, buckling as the pain of the shot finally caught up with me. With his arm wrapped around my waist and my right arm across his shoulder, I watched as Kacey walked to the open doorway and called for help.

Resting my head on the gurney I now lay on, I looked through the open doorway of room eight, watching Kacey who stood in front of the reception, currently talking with an older man dressed in a suit. I could only guess the male was the lead detective for the crime scene, because that's what this place was now, a crime scene.

"This is for the pain."

The female paramedic tapped the crook of my elbow before inserting the tube of a drip beneath my skin. My jeans had started to tighten around my thigh moments ago, the pain pulsing, sharpening, and burning hotter with each minute that passed. The paramedic had explained that blood was pooling beneath my skin and although I had nothing to worry about as the bullet had missed my femur and femoral artery, they still needed to get me to the hospital as soon as possible.

"Thank you." I gave her a weak smile, before wrapping the blanket they had given me tighter around myself.

"Nicole Saunders?"

I looked up to find the detective had stopped in the doorway of the room, notepad in hand. He was older, his brown hair greying at the temples, with a pleasant face. Kind green eyes were accompanied by small smile lines which crinkled at their corners.

"I'm Detective Smith. I realize this has been a traumatic day for you so I will keep this brief, but I just have a couple of questions I need to ask?"

I nodded, my focus flitting to Ty and Kay who stood out on the parking lot, watching us.

"At what point did you become aware that your friend, Jayne Phillips, was missing?"

"When I went back to our Motel room, number twelve, this morning."

"At what time was that, roughly?"

"Around ten, I think."

The female paramedic moved behind the gurney. A click sounded. The detective glanced at her and nodded, before moving out onto the walkway. I was slowly wheeled out of the room.

In daylight, the Creek Motel looked harmless, dare I say welcoming, but the flash of red and blue lights sweeping across the exterior from the multiple cop cars that now consumed the car lot was a sobering reminder of why the last few hours had been possibly the worst of my life.

My gaze moved to the trio of cops that walked through the doorway of the reception, each carrying a segment of the computer from the office to the trunk of one of the cars. Detaining the evidence, because that's what it was after all—key evidence in the murder of three of our friends; proof that Ty had reason to shoot Ernie; that Sarah did indeed shoot me; and proof that Jayne wasn't the first victim of the Motel owners' son.

My friends were dead because I had asked them to come to some stupid festival for the weekend. Jayne was dead because I had abandoned her.

"And when you say 'your room', would I be correct in guessing you were sharing a room with Miss Phillips?" the detective continued, falling in step alongside my gurney.

Tears filled my eyes. "Yes, that's right."

"According to Mister Hudson and Mister Grant, you came to their room in the early hours of the morning?"

Heat licked my cheeks at the idea of what this man could be thinking. To make matters worse, his team would get a good show once they reviewed the CCTV footage from last night. Heat travelled down my neck. I moved my focus to my lap and settled on a slow nod, before adding, "I was unable to sleep because Tyler and I had a disagreement earlier last night. I could hear Ty and Kay talking and I felt bad, so I decided to sort it out with him. My mother always says never go to sleep on an argument."

The detective nodded and scribbled something in his notepad. "What time was that at?"

"Just after three."

"Instead of going back to your room after you and

Mister Hudson had made peace, you stayed in Mister Hudson's and Mister Grant's room for the remainder of the night. Is that correct?"

My cheeks burned hotter, so much so that the tears in my eyes, tears that wanted to fall, seemed to have dried up. "That's right."

As we drew closer to one of the ambulances, my paramedic carefully manoeuvred the gurney around so that I was facing the motel. My entire body went numb at the sight of a black body bag being wheeled out of room one.

"Jayne." Her name trembled from my lips.

"So you mentioned that you went back to your room at roughly ten this morning. On entering the room, did you find any evidence of a struggle?"

Bile coated my tongue and tears spilled from my eyes as the image of her thrashing on the bed beneath George slammed into my mind.

My throat restricted. I watched as the men wheeled Jayne's body across the lot to join the other four body bags which lay on the ground.

"The bed sheets on Jayne's side were a mess, but no. Nothing indicated any struggle, but my concern worsened after I found that she wasn't in the bathroom or even hiding in the wardrobe. I had to unlock the door to get into the room—"

"Had you locked it the night before?"

"Yes, and clearly, it had stayed locked. All the windows in the rooms are welded down so I didn't understand how she could have gotten out."

I explained what had happened detail for detail, not wanting to leave anything out. I told him how Sarah had made some silly excuses when we had asked if she had seen Jayne, how she'd acted as if no one else had come with the three of us. I told him how once I had been allowed to go into the office to use their landline, Sarah had excused herself for some reason and that was when I'd noticed the computer screen was showing footage of not only the outside of the Motel, but inside the rooms, and that was how I saw the man who Sarah claimed was their son, George; how I saw Jayne's case was in his room and I became frightened for my friend, and troubled at the fact that Sarah had told us we were the only ones in the Motel.

"I haven't trusted her since the moment we checked in."

A male paramedic joined the female and together, they manoeuvred me and the gurney into the back of the ambulance.

The detective nodded thoughtfully. "So, after Mrs. Dodd came back and you explained you were unable to get through to Jayne's mobile, then what?"

I couldn't understand why he was asking me all of this. I was sure both Kacey and Tyler had already told him everything, but then I guess he just wanted to be sure, to see if our stories matched up. The CCTV footage would at least cement our story.

"So you went back to check the footage while Shauna and Craig caused a distraction?"

"I knew that the footage would show us what happened the night before. If Jayne had left, then we would have left to find her, but what we saw..." I took a shuddering breath. "That man... George, he raped and murdered her, and then he dragged her body through a trap door inside the wardrobe." Fresh tears fell down my cheeks.

"That will be all, Miss Saunders," he said gently.

I wiped at my face. "Sarah said he was her son. That he was ill?"

The detective flipped his notepad closed and placed it, along with his pen, in his inside jacket pocket. "At the moment, we don't know if that is indeed the case. My team are searching the entire motel and will collect all relevant documents. If the male is indeed suffering from some form of illness, well, this was not the right place for him to be cared for."

"What will happen to her?"

"Hard to say without looking at the evidence. Mister Hudson mentioned that she had confessed to other such events in the past, which if she has indeed witnessed assault and murder on numerous occassions without reporting them, then she is an accomplice to murder; attempted murder toward yourself; abuse in regards to her son's wellbeing, and then recording guests without their permission is an invasion of privacy." He folded his arms across his chest. "To put it in a nutshell, Miss Saunders, if you and your friends are willing to testify, then there is enough here to make sure she goes to prison for a long time."

"Good." Life imprisonment didn't even seem enough for what had gone on here. How many other people had lost their lives?

"But you have time to think about that. That's all I need from you at the moment, but if there is anything else, I will be in contact."

"Okay, Detective. Thank you."

A scream pierced the afternoon sky. The shrill,

agonizing sound made the hairs at the back of my neck stand on end.

"Excuse me." The detective made his way across the lot to the other ambulance, which I could only presume contained Sarah.

"Is she okay?" Tyler appeared at the back of the ambulance, Kacey by his side.

"She's very lucky," the paramedic replied.

"I'm lucky to be shot at?"

"You're lucky that the shot was at a distance, but more so that it has landed at the back of your right thigh. As I stated earlier, the bullet missed your femur and major artery. Nevertheless, the hit has caused some heavy bleeding so we need to get you to the hospital." The woman looked between them. "Does one of you want to come with her?"

"Where's my boy?" Sarah shouted. "What have they done to my boy?"

"You still got my keys, Nikki?" Kay asked while looking over his shoulder at the other ambulance.

I reached into my left pocket and pulled out the keys; throwing them to Tyler.

"You go with her, Ty. I will follow." Turning back to me, he winked. "I'll see you at the hospital, alright?"

"Yeah." I gave him a weak smile.

Grabbing his keys, Kacey disappeared from sight, and Tyler climbed into the back of the ambulance, taking the free seat by my side. He fastened himself in and then took hold of my hand. "You okay?"

"I've been better."

The paramedic locked the doors and moved to the

other seat. "Ready when you are, Jim."

The engine started.

"I'm sorry."

"For what?"

"For this weekend. Kay and I... we just wanted to cheer you up."

I turned my hand over so I could hold his.

"I don't regret agreeing to this weekend away." I lowered my voice. "I don't regret last night. I just regret..." I swiped at my eyes, my focus fixed on our entwined hands. "I regret that I left Jayne alone. If I'd have been there, we could have fought him off. I could have called for you and Kay. She could still be alive if I'd have just stayed put instead of being selfish—"

"My boy!" Sarah's voice was a shrill, raw cry. "No, no, not my boy."

Muffled voices replied, but I couldn't make them out over the soft growl of the ambulance's engine or the crunch of gravel beneath its big wheels

"Or that bastard could have hurt you, too." He lifted our hands and placed a kiss on mine. "We weren't to know that any of this would happen."

"No, but this place has given me the creeps since we got here, and Sarah, as soon as I met her—"

"No one expect this shit to ever happen. Jayne was locked in her room. Anyone would think they were safe. No one would expect there to be a secret way in and—"

"That bitch! What did she do to him? What did she do?"

"Ignore her." Tyler squeezed my hand. "She's gone.

This place is gone. We never have to see her or it again."

"We will if we testify against her." My focus fixed on the locked, double metal doors. Sarah's wails penetrated through the thick material, turning my stomach.

The ambulance curved left and as it moved onto the road, sirens began to ring, drowning out everything else but our voices.

"If we testify, we help put her away, but from what Detective Smith has said, they have enough on her to put her in a cell and throw away the key without our word in court."

The idea of standing up in front of a room of people and having to talk through the last twenty-four hours made me nauseous, but I would do it. I would do it if it meant justice for Jayne, Shauna, and Craig. I wanted to be there, to see and hear the judgment passed on Sarah.

"Try and get some rest." He cupped my cheek and, leaning forward, pressed a kiss to my temple.

"If I'd have lost either of you..." My throat closed over as I looked into his eyes.

"You haven't, and no matter what happens in the future, you won't. Ever."

Placing my hand on top of his, I leant in and kissed him. "I love you, Ty."

His smile was soft, a little sad. "You love us both."

I sighed and pressed my head against his. "I do. In different ways, and I'm sorry. I wish—"

"It's okay. It's enough. For me, it's enough." He kissed me again, before pulling away. "Now sleep."

My chest clenched at the sadness in his eyes. "Ty—?"

"When you wake up, we will be at the hospital with Kay." He squeezed my hand. "I promise I won't leave your side, but you should try and get some sleep."

I nodded. "Okay."

Resting my head on the gurney, I took a deep breath and closed my eyes.

Epilogue

Wichita, Kansas
Five months later

"And are you still having the dreams?"

"I've been having a new one.

"Tell me about it."

"I'm running across the parking lot and I trip, landing face first in the dirt. As I go to push myself up, someone grabs my ankles. I glance over my shoulder and it's Craig. He has a huge bullet hole in his head, blood pouring down his deathly white face, and his eyes are bloodshot. He has a tight hold of my legs and he says, 'Where do you think you're going?' And the next minute, he is dragging me back toward the motel. I'm kicking and screaming, my nails are digging into the dirt as I try and pull myself forward..."

"Then what?"

"He pulls me into one of the rooms and throws me on the bed. I go to push myself up, but this shadowy figure jumps on me and the next thing I know, the lamp is switched on and it's Kacey. And I calm down...."

"You jerk."

A grin curls his mouth, before he leans down and kisses me. His hands go to my thighs which he pushes apart. My eyes flutter shut. My hands are busy moving up his naked back, not stopping until my fingers entwine in his hair. I groan as he tears my panties off me, and without warning, he thrusts inside me.

My breathing grows heavy and as the first slither of moans escapes me, his hand covers my mouth. I open my eyes and it's not Kacey I'm looking at. It's *him*. His eyes are wild and frantic, and I start thrashing, but he keeps going; thrusting, hard and brutal. Tears fill my eyes and sick fills my mouth, but I can't get him off me.

I glance to the side and Ernie is standing there with a video camera in his hand and... the sick bastard is masturbating.

"Are you ready for me?"

I look over his shoulder and Tyler stands at the end of the bed, we roll and I'm on top, only when I look down, it's Jayne. My hand is across her mouth, her legs around my hips, and her eyes are wide, terrified.

I scramble off her, falling to the floor, and the wardrobe door swings open. Shauna climbs through. She's naked and her neck is purple and black and she is crawling toward me.

"Is it my turn?" she asks.

Then the door to the room swings open and in walks Sarah with a shotgun.

" 'Little whore.' She spits and then fires."

"And then you wake up?"

I looked up at Melissa, my psychiatrist, and just nodded.

"Do you remember what I told you when you first came to see me?"

"That I feel guilty."

"You feel that somehow, your friend's deaths are

your fault. By seeing yourself in the position of your friend's killer, you are still seeing yourself as the guilty party, but are you responsible for the actions of others, Nicole?"

I swiped at the tears on my cheeks. "No."

"What you went through, what you saw, was awful, but your friends died at the hands of mentally unstable individuals. Individuals who almost killed you."

Thanks to Sarah's shot, I had ended up with minor muscle damage in my right thigh, and although on the odd cold and rainy day it hurt like hell, and I found myself with a lovely scar and the inability to walk fantastically uphill, my leg was healed. Tyler, on the other hand, had hit Sarah right in her femur, meaning she had gone through major surgery to get her leg back to a decent condition. Unfortunately, the massive amount of blood she had lost hadn't killed her and instead, she had been given forty-five years in prison— for attempted murder on me, for being an accessory to murder, for neglect and abuse of her son, and for voyeurism.

Tyler, Kacey, and I had testified and watched and listened as the prosecution delivered their verdict, and although the motel owner was locked up on the other side of the state, I still couldn't forget the way she'd looked at me as she was taken away, a deadly promise in her glacial eyes.

She wanted me dead.

A small buzzer went off.

"That's our session finished for today." Taking out a small sheet of blue paper, she scribbled something down. "I'm going to up your medication. Hopefully, this will help you sleep a little better, but every time you start feeling this guilt, every time you wake up from that dream, I want you to take a deep breath and say your mantra." She handed me the piece of paper. "Will you say it for me now, Nicole?"

I scrubbed my hands across my face and laughed to myself.

"I am not responsible for the actions of others." I dropped my hands to my lap. "What happened in Silver Creek..." The memory of five black body bags lay on the ground of the motel car lot flashed in my mind.

"Was?" she prompted.

"...Was not my fault." I looked up at her.

She arched her eyebrow. "And what happened..."

"What happened in Silver Creek...Stays in Silver Creek."

THE END?

Also by Elizabeth Morgan

Scottish Werewolves: freaky Vampires and a Slayer with a bad addiction and an insane legacy. Add a big dose of sarcasm, sizzling chemistry; a lot of silver and a ton of blood and . . . Welcome to the Blood Series.

She-Wolf
(Blood Series: Prequel)

Cranberry Blood
(Blood Series: Book One)

Available from most online retailers.
Also available in print.

www.e-morgan.com/the-blood-series.html

Standalone

Razel Dazzle
A modern twist on a long haired tale....

A modern re-telling of the fairytale Rapunzel.

FREE to download from most online retailers. Also available in print.

For more information on Elizabeth's work, published and upcoming, head on over to her site: http://www.e-morgan.com

Acknowledgement

The re-release of this book wouldn't have been possible without the help of Zee Monodee, my fabulous editor and friend who is a constant source of support for me, and who has helped me whip this book into shape. Thanks for everything, hun. You're a star.

A big thank you to Elaina Lee who designed the gritty, sexy, amazing cover. I love it so much. Thank you.

And my readers, old and new, thank you for taking a chance on my work. Thank you for your support, your comments, and your reviews; just thank you. You are truly wonderful, and I hope from the bottom of my heart that you continue to trust in my creative insanity and enjoy my stories.

About the Author

Elizabeth Morgan is a multi-published author of urban fantasy, paranormal, erotic horror, f/f, and contemporary; all with a degree of romance, a dose of action and a hit of sarcasm, sizzle or blood, but you can be sure that no matter what the genre, Elizabeth always manages to give a unique and often humorous spin to her stories.

Like her tagline says; A pick 'n' mix genre author. "I'm not greedy. I just like variety."

And that she does, so look out for more information on her upcoming releases at her website: www.e-morgan.com

Away from the computer, Elizabeth can be found in the garden trying hard not to kill her plants, dancing around her little cottage with the radio on while she cleans, watching movies or good television programmes – Dr Who? Atlantis? The Musketeers? Poldark? American Horror Story? Heck, yes! – Or curled up with her two cats reading a book.

Where to find Elizabeth Online:

Website:
www.e-morgan.com
Blog:
www.xxxxmyworldxxxx.blogspot.co.uk
Twitter:
@EMorgan2010
Goodreads:
http://www.goodreads.com/ElizabethMorgan
Facebook:
http://www.facebook.com/elizabeth.morgan.944
Pinterest:
http://www.pinterest.com/elizabethm2012/boards/
TSU:
https://www.tsu.co/ElizabethMorgan
Zazzle:
http://www.zazzle.co.uk/elizabeth_morgan

Made in the USA
Columbia, SC
28 July 2018